THE PEEPHOLE

MIRIKA MAYO CORNELIUS

THE PEEPHOLE

An Akirim Press Publishing
Book Cover by Akirim Press/Mirika Mayo Cornelius
www.akirimpress.com

<u>Acknowledgements</u>

I first and always thank God for the giving of his Son, Jesus, to save me, and I acknowledge and confess that without Him, I have and am nothing.

To my husband and son – I love and thank you.

To my parents and siblings – I love you all.

mirikacornelius.com

THE PEEPHOLE

When a hopeful, widowed mother and her teenage daughter move into a brand new home, they are unaware of the violent, hidden history that took place on the property a long time ago. It is this history that begins to brutally stalk their every movement because it refuses to share a space with any newcomers.

If the small family refuses to leave their new residence fast enough, they, too, may mysteriously vanish like those who dared to stay before them.

TABLE OF CONTENTS

THE PEEPHOLE

THE PEEPHOLE

CHAPTER 1

"Mama, I'm going to step outside for a little bit. Is that alright?" asked the slim yet muscular teenage girl as she eagerly glanced out of their new living room window at the fresh scenery.

Her mother looked up from unpacking the smallest box from the multitude of boxes that the movers were unloading. "Alright. Stay close because this is a new area, and we don't know anybody. I mean it, Dina," she sternly ordered. "Stay close."

"Okay," Dina stressed, rolling her eyes slightly but understanding her mother's perspective - the safe perspective. "I'll be back inside as soon as the movers are finished bringing the stuff in. I just want to check out the view."

"No boys!"

"Ma!" she looked back, stunned her mother would mindlessly embarrass her in front of the group of guys bringing in the boxes. One of them cracked a smile, amused by her slight humiliation, so she moved from the steps of the condominium quickly and started to wander off a bit.

It was a fairly busy street, and after watching a woman walk back and forth to get groceries from her car, she was glad her mom was able to find lower level condos. The condos were attached to each other via a small corridor, and each front door faced the other, however some condominiums were built slightly different. It appeared as if the architects wanted to design something more unique. Each door of the burnt red brick condos was painted a different color, some of the entrances facing the street. It was odd, but it worked as a natural mood booster for the neighborhood. It even made Dina smile, making her feel like she was walking around in an enchanted story book.

There was a lengthy row of trees equidistant apart. The leaves all had red tips, but there were no blooms. She was thankful because she was highly allergic to flowers, and she wasn't looking forward to being miserable during the Spring and Summer months.

"Dina!" her mom called from inside their new home causing her to run back inside.

"Yeah, ma?" she answered while hanging on to the outside of the doorway.

"Your boxes are already inside your room. I need you to go ahead and get your stuff situated how you want so we can go out and get something to eat later," she stated before one of the movers politely interjected.

"It's not my business but the restaurant down the street makes a mean carryout special on Mondays. Look up Mays & Belles. It's the only one in the city. Full menu and all."

"You live on this side?" her mother asked.

"Actually, I do live here. Not here as in here in this neighborhood," he pointed to the floor, "but on this side of the city. My wife loved the peacefulness of this side of town versus the hustle and noise of the north side."

"I agree." She looked at Dina. "I told you it was going to be a great move." Then, she looked back at the mover. "And thank you, sir. I will definitely take a load off tonight and possibly order that carryout from Mays & Belles."

He wiped his face with a white rag, smiled and walked back outside. Her mother turned to her with a big grin on her face. "See. Things are going great already. We won't eat pizza after all."

"Good. We've been eating that entirely too much lately, Grace."

"Alright," her mother stated firmly, glaring at her. "Don't play with me child. You'll never be my mother, so you won't call me by my first name, understand?"

Dina stuck her neck out and stretched her eyes jokingly. "I'm just playin'. I wanted to get your reaction."

"Well, don't do that anymore because I might really react. Understand?"

"Of course I do, Ma." She walked over and gave her mother a kiss on the cheek before proceeding to her new bedroom. It was much bigger than her previous, so the amount of items in the boxes weren't nearly enough to fill the space, but that was fine by her because she didn't want her room crowded. She planned on using the extra space to work out and prepare for track season while also practicing her music. She was a pianist, but she fell in love with the keyboard, so her mother decided to leave the piano with Dina's grandmother instead of hauling it and risk damage. Dina would instead have a brand new keyboard delivered to the condo. There was just enough space for it, and that was all Dina really needed and wanted.

By the evening, Dina and her mother were exhausted, but the doorbell rang just in time before they became faint from hunger pains. She'd gotten the number for that restaurant before the mover left, and ordered what she hoped would be some great food.

"Next time we may need to stop at a grocery store before moving in so we will have food in the fridge, Ma."

"Good idea, but this was our first time moving, so my planning was off. We ordered enough for leftovers in case we get hungry over night, and the water is on, so we can't complain too much."

"And we have lights."

"Amen! Do you remember when they cut our lights off accidently when we were in the other place?"

"Ma, I won't forget that, ever," she agreed, rolling her eyes at the thought of it all. She remembered that her mom was in the middle of making a pound cake when the lights suddenly went out. The entire cake flattened. Meanwhile, Dina was in the shower when everything went pitch black, and because she was still a bit spooked of the dark at the age of fifteen, her screams could not have been loud enough through her vividly haunting imagination. It took them all night to get to the lights turned back on when her mother helped the electric company discover their mistake.

Dina's mother got up from the sofa and verified it was the delivery service through the window before going to answer the door.

"Here, Ma, you left the money on the box," Dina called, noticing that her mother left the money for the food on a box. She rushed the money to her mother as the food was being passed through the doorway. When the delivery driver left the door, Dina shut it and followed his path through the peephole. "Cool."

"What?"

"Never had one before. It looks odd on the other side."

"Oh, that little peephole. Yeah, this is your first time looking through one, huh? Just make sure you use it. Don't open that door for anyone out here. We don't know these people yet."

"Mom, I'm almost grown," she expressed, plopping down next to her mother to explore the food in the plastic containers.

"Even when you're grown, check the peephole, but don't open the door if the other side is unfamiliar, and I mean that, Dina.

Consider everyone over here unfamiliar until I tell you otherwise. Now let's eat so we can go to sleep."

With her mother in the master bedroom and Dina in the other, the night ended in full stomachs and a need for a great night's sleep. Because her mother labeled the boxes, they were able to locate the sheets easily. Before midnight, they were both lightly snoring without a care in the world. However, in the middle of the night, at around two-thirty A.M., Dina began coughing, possibly due to reflux. It was normal for her to have if she ate too late before lying down, therefore, she got up and dragged herself to the kitchen for a glass of water.

It was dark in the condo, and she tried to remember where all the boxes were located so she wouldn't fall over and hurt herself. She didn't want to turn on the light to awaken her mother, so she tipped extra carefully, only knocking one box in the process. When she entered the kitchen, she rubbed her hand above the stove to flick on the stove light, but she hit the fan on accident.

"Shoot!" she whispered before flicking on the light and tapping the fan off . Then, she turned on the faucet, grabbed her cup and filled it up. As she shut the water off, she heard something from outside, like it was at the door. At first, she ignored it, but when she heard the shuffling again, she tipped around to the front door to check on what or who it may be.

She walked to the peephole, almost in glee at her first time truly having to use it. The noises got louder, and she halted, scared that someone was trying to get into her house, but suddenly, the noise stopped. Immediately, she pounced to the door and peered through the hole. No one was there.

Dina stepped away, considering that she may have been half asleep, despite the goosebumps covering her arms. She turned to walk back to her room, only standing still briefly in the middle of the floor to drink some of the water down, before there was a tremendous bang on the door. The sound startled her so much that she wasted some of the water, even choking as she spun around to face the door.

"Dina?"

At the sound of her name, Dina became so startled that she dropped her cup of water onto the floor. It was her mother.

"Dina!" her mom exclaimed as she watched her daughter's drink topple to the floor. "What is the matter? Are you alright? I heard you coughing…"

"Yeah," she interjected, glancing back at the door. "Yeah, I choked on the water. Sorry, I was trying not to wake you up. Did you hear that noise?"

"The only thing I heard was you coughing. You know I can hear you through the thunder and the rain. You're my baby. Are you sure you're okay?" she asked, patting Dina on the back. "You sound so shaken up, but I know choking will do that to you. Having bouts of reflux again, aren't you?" she asked without waiting on Dina to answer. "I'll stop and get some apple cider vinegar tomorrow on my way back home from orientation. That should help. Go on back to bed."

"But you didn't hear that noise? It was loud. When I was getting water, there was movement right outside the door. Next thing I know, somebody or something hit the door just now. That's how loud it was. It wasn't a regular knock."

"Lemme see. Did you look?" she asked, moving her daughter out of the way to go toward the door. She put her ear up to the door before peering through the peephole. "I don't see anyone." Then, she opened the door.

"Mom!" she shouted, afraid for her to open the door in the middle of the night.

"Shh!" her mom hushed her, quieting Dina by waving her hand. She opened the door slowly and looked out. There was no one and no noise, so she shut and locked it. "It was probably a dog or some animal to be honest, baby. As long as it's not inside with us, we're fine. Whatever it was can stay out. Come on. Let's go back to bed."

She passed by Dina as she stood there staring at the door in the darkness before cleaning her mess and going back to bed.

CHAPTER 2

The morning came in with much delight, and Dina's mother was already gone. She left a note telling Dina that she wouldn't forget the apple cider vinegar and that she would bring home some of their favorites from the grocery store. There was twenty dollars left next to the letter so she could use it to buy lunch from any of the fast food places down the block.

Dina walked into the bathroom to take a shower, and when she looked in the mirror, she noticed the red smear of her mother's lipstick on her cheek.

"Figures," she whispered to herself, wishing her mom would have awakened her instead of slipping out quietly. Any other time she would have heard her, but Dina had spent most of the night attempting to hear more noises at the front door again. It never happened, so she ended up falling into a deep sleep.

After showering, Dina swallowed some of her leftover food down for breakfast, found the radio and tuned in to the stations to see what would be going on during the week as she started un-boxing living room and kitchen accessories like paintings, pictures and vases to decorate the home. She pulled the curtains back to let more of the sunshine into her new home. Everything brightened up perfectly as the rays drew brand new horizons over her head atop the ceiling and traced their way down the pearly white dining room walls. The more sights and sounds she saw and heard, from birds chirping to the soar of airline flights across the sky, the more at home she felt in the new atmosphere.

She wasn't an hour into decorating that there was an unexpected knock on the door. Turning down the music, she took a deep breath, hopped over the boxes and went to answer. As she placed her hand on the knob, she abruptly removed it.

"Check the peephole, Dina," she sang, remembering her mother's wise words. "You never know who's on the other side." She peered through the hole, but no one was there. Therefore, she quickly, she ran to the window to see if she simply missed who it was or if it was children playing around. School was out for the summer, so it was likely that some playful children lived in the area and wanted to make the new people crazy for the day as a formal introduction to the Cloverton neighborhood. However, when she searched outside through the window, no one was there.

She stood back and thought about things for a second, before she heard another knock. Instead of going to the door this time, she hollered, "Who is it?" There was no answer, so she approached the door frustrated but cautious, picking up a large brass figurine her mom won at an auction to defend herself if need be. "Stop playing at the door!"

Growing more frustrated by the second because no one was responding, she didn't even look through the peephole, but swung the door open with the brass figurine in launch position.

Again, no one was there – to the front and neither the right or left. Across from her was the next condo, and from what she knew, it was empty, proven by the management combination lock attached to the knob of the rusted brown door.

Confused but satisfied that she didn't have to defend herself from any intruder, she shut the door and one last time, looked out of the peephole. The door across from them was no longer that rusted brown color but a bright orange-yellow, like the color of the sun in children's story books.

"What the??"

Yanking the door back open, her eyes instantly fell on the door across from her which was oddly brown once again. She blinked her eyes in total disbelief that the door was orange-yellowish when she saw it from inside the house. Therefore, she quickly shut the door again and looked through the peephole.

"Brown. Just like I thought. Must have been the sunlight causing it, coming in from a weird angle. Cool though." She moved away from the door, still pondering over who was knocking. "And I can see right now that these people around here play too much." She turned back around to face the room of boxes and decided to hit the road instead of tackling them at that moment. She was going for a walk with that twenty dollars her mom left her in order to get something to eat for lunch later.

Dina grabbed her sunglasses and pulled her dark brown hair up directly on top of her head so that it created an awesome, puffy fro, and then, she left the condo, double checking the lock on the door twice since it was obvious that someone was toying with them.

Once she hit the pavement, she lifted her arms, stretched to loosen up and decided to jog. She hadn't run in three days which was too long, and she definitely didn't want to get out of shape for track.

There were some small children already out playing what looked to be the game of Tag, and as she jogged further down the road, she inconspicuously glanced at a couple of teenage boys that were on the corner talking. They saw her, but she pretended to not see them by gracefully looking away. As she turned the corner, she ran into a few more people her age, females this time. She ran past them as she smiled and spoke before entering into the independently owned café. They sold salads, coffee and bagels along with other treats according to the colorful posters on the windows, so her stomach was ready to take it all in.

The aroma of various breads and meats aroused her senses and left her wanting to taste everything, so she drifted to the counter to get a closer look at the menu and order. She took out her twenty dollar bill, folded and unfolded it a couple times before deciding to get the full twenty dollars worth of food that included two slices of pie, the second of which she would give to her mother.

"Thank you," she stated as the cashier rang her up. She took her ticket and sat down on a small, fancy purple bench with wrought iron legs and wooden back which was located near the entrance of the café in order to wait until they called her number. While she sat enjoying the presence of her fellow neighbors, someone sat down beside her. It was one of the guys she passed by on the way to the café. She identified him from the corner of her eye, but she pretended she didn't see him because he was quite cute which made her extremely nervous.

"I saw you jogging out there. You new?"

Dina glanced over as if she didn't know he was talking to her. Immediately, her face felt flushed. "Me? Yeah, yes...I just moved in, me and my mom."

"I'm Michael, but people who I introduce myself to can call me Mike."

Dina laughed. "Is that not automatic? Most people resort to Mike with the name Michael anyway?"

"I won't answer them though," he smiled, "Unless it's you. What's your name?"

Dina laughed at his silly, flirtatious line and replied, "Dina. People I tell my name can call me Dina though," she joked.

"Not Diane."

"No way," she laughed. "Dina, please. Just Dina." Just then, her receipt number was called, and she excused herself from the conversation to collect her food. By the time she made it back over to the bench, Michael was already standing, ready to walk her out. He appeared to be about six feet six inches tall, but he was possibly shorter by a couple inches because the sneakers he had on gave him a boost.

"Do you mind?"

"No, I don't mind," she replied as he opened the door for her.

"May I walk you home? I won't come in or try to, just want to walk you back."

"No, I don't mind walking back home with you. Did you grow up here?"

"Yeah. Been right here in this same spot all my life. I know just about everyone pretty well on this block right here, except for you."

"What would you like to know?"

"First thing is if you have a man because if you do, I have to change my goals in this conversation," he laughed, "so I won't look stupid later."

"How will you look stupid?"

"Well, if I happen to like you, then I don't want to be shut down when I ask to come hang out with you some time. Maybe meet at this same café," he said, turning back to point at the small restaurant, "and let me fill that empty stomach."

"And if you don't like me?"

"Well, I'll see you in school, in passing, if I'm not running in the opposite direction."

Dina laughed, "How old are you?"

"I'm eighteen. It's my last year at ..."

"Spark High?"

He glanced at her and smiled, happy they were going to be at the same school. "Yeah. I'm assuming you asked me that because that's where you'll be starting."

"Yep."

"I figured. What grade?"

"Eleventh. I'm seventeen. My birthday is in January."

"I just turned eighteen last month."

"Really?"

"Yeah."

His voice was deep, and Dina was falling into it every time he spoke. He had a nice low afro that was tapered on the sides, and his teeth were perfectly white. He had a scar on his right arm that was revealed because he wore a jersey which sparked her to ask...

"You play ball?"

"Basketball is my thing. As a matter of fact, I was on my way to the court until I saw you. I had to detour."

Dina blushed and quickly changed the subject. "Where's the gym?"

"Oh, there's no gym close by, but the court is a couple blocks that way," he pointed. "You ball?"

"No, but I can. I run track. Is the team any good? I know the school used to have good sprinters until the best ones graduated."

"Our track team. It's okay. If you're fast, they could use your help. I'm sure they won't pass on you. Your grades good?"

"Of course."

"Well then, you're probably in already."

"You think?"

"I mean," he replied as he popped his jersey from his chest. "You can't outrun your boy right here. You might be about ten steps behind. That's still fast enough."

"What? Just you wait."

"Bet."

"Leaving you in the dust."

"If I let you."

"Let? Oh you have confidence for someone who doesn't know a thing about my skills on the track."

"I *chose* basketball. I used to run track, but stopped early on."

"Why not do both?"

"Basketball is my love. I'm already accepted academically into some colleges, and I'm thinking I can land a full ride with basketball. If not, my academics will do it. I'm trying to keep everything on the up and up, so my family won't be burdened with me needing them for finances."

"You sound like me." She looked up, and they were already at her condo. "I'm here."

"Here?" he asked, shocked as he gawked at the place before taking a couple of steps back. "Right here? This is where you live?"

"Yeah. I see you looking confused or something?" she said as she took her keys out of her pocket.

"No, no, I'm not confused. It's just that nobody has lived here in a while is all. Which one you live in?" he asked, looking at the condo opposite hers.

"Not the one you're eyeballing. It's this one. So do you like?"

"What?" he asked startled. "Oh yeah, yeah, it's a nice place to live. Mine looks the same way," he laughed nervously.

"No, Mike. I'm talking about me. Do you like me?"

Suddenly, he remembered what he said on his walk back and replied, "Yeah, yeah, I like you. My mistake. You got me nervous."

"I see that," she said, tracing his eyes back up to the other condo. "Can I ask you a question before you go?"

"Shoot."

"Why do you keep looking up there like that? I can tell you're bothered."

"Hey, Michael!" someone called, and Michael turned around to see who it was. It was one of his teammates ready to head to the court. Michael turned back to her. "What's your number?"

"Can you remember it?"

"Honestly, when you give it to me, you see that basketball over there?" he asked, pointing to the basketball in his friend's hand.

"Yeah.

"I'm writing it on my ball in permanent ink. I'll never lose it. If I put it on paper or in my head, it's gone," he laughed. "What I remember, I keep on my fingertips." Dina smiled, impressed by his flirtatious way with words, and he continued. "What is it? I'll call you. Promise."

Dina told him her number, and he gave her his. Then, he ran off. Dina didn't stand there and watch. She walked to her front door while rehearsing his phone number. As soon as she went inside, she tossed the food down on the chair and scribbled his number down on the fast food bag. Immediately, however, she felt like someone was directly behind her. She threw the pen down and swung her arm to defend herself, but no one was there.

"Close the door, Dina," she reminded herself as she marched over to the door to shut and lock it. "I have to do better." As soon as she shut the door, there was a sound behind it. She looked out of the peephole, and what she saw made her stumble backwards over the boxes in the living room and onto to the floor.

Although shaken, she got up quickly, collecting herself, and briskly walked closer to the door. From a short distance, she strained to look inside the peephole, but she couldn't see anything at all, so she slowly approached with full apprehension until there they were again.

Placing her palms gently against the door, she balanced her weight easily as not to disturb the people she watched on the other side, but the people weren't on the other side of the door. They were somehow inside the peephole. Awestruck, she watched them move about in their own little world, and they actually fit inside, almost like they were in another dimension yet right in front of her.

There were two cute children, a little, fat-cheeked, brown-skinned boy and a thin little girl who looked just like the boy. They were possibly fraternal twins. There was also a lady whom Dina assumed was their mother. She was laughing herself to tears as she fell into whom Dina assumed to be her husband's muscular arms. He was a tall, naturally well-built man, and she was a tall lady as well who appeared very healthy and joyous. The children embraced their father's legs like they were large tree branches, trying to swing on them until he picked the children up and tickled them until they could take it no more. Although the scene would have made anyone smile, it didn't bring a smile to Dina's face. Instead, she'd become completely perplexed.

Taking a deep breath, she placed her hand upon the door knob, in disbelief at what she was seeing, and quickly swung the door open. There was no one there. Terrified, she shut it, falling back against it, totally feeling like she was being pranked. Was someone watching her and playing one big joke or was everything she saw real? Her heart raced. She felt stuck in place, her own apprehension holding her hostage.

"You're dreaming. No one's there. Peepholes don't do that. They don't play movies," she whispered under her breath, finally convincing herself to turn around once more to peer inside the old, rundown peculiar peephole. When she did, there was no one there anymore. "Oh thank God!" She fell back against the door again. She immediately wanted to call her mom's job, but decided against it. "This isn't an emergency though, is it? It can wait," she told herself as she went and grabbed the food, put the pies in the refrigerator, and escaped back to her bedroom to eat and get some sleep, assuming that she was stressed and needed some relaxation after the move. She remained asleep until her mother returned.

"Asleep so early?" her mom asked as she opened Dina's bedroom door and then rushed into her bedroom to undress and put on something ugly and comfortable. Both Dina and her mother firmly believed that the ugliest fashions are the most comfortable, all the way down to pajamas. Their rule was to only wear ugly clothes inside the house at night to calm the mood, so they would dress in the tackiest, most worn clothing to enjoy the night.

"Oh, hey, mom," she sat up, with half of her food still beside her in the bed. "I bought you a pie and a bowl of salad. It's in the fridge."

"Hey, baby. Will you do me a favor and go out to the car. I have a couple more grocery bags in there with a couple six packs of organic soda? Thanks for the salad and the pie, too, sweetheart."

"Okay," Dina replied, stretching and suddenly recalling what happened to her earlier. "Mom, I think I was really tired today. I thought I saw people walking around and playing in the peephole."

Her mom stopped removing her work clothes. "Were people outside of the door?"

"No. I mean, I don't think so. I mean, inside the peephole...really."

"Dina," she finally stated, dismissing the conversation as too odd for her to deal with. "Baby, just run outside and get my bags. I wanna get ugly after this long day, okay? I'll whip up some spaghetti, and that will last for two days so that I can get a break before I start seeing things like you. Next month, we have to work on getting you your driver's license and save up for a car so you can take care of more stuff while I'm at work."

"I told you a long time ago that I should have already tried for my license, but no," she sang until her mom gave her a stern look. "Okay, I'm going, I'm going." Dina slipped on her shoes, grabbed the car keys and went outside. The evening had come in cooler than it was earlier that day, and the shadows from the trees intersected her body as she walked to the trunk of the car to collect the bags. As she shut it, someone called her name. She turned around to see Michael who stood with his arms out like she should have seen him as soon as she stepped outside.

Feeling a bit embarrassed because she didn't check her hair before coming out of the house, she simply answered his call with a wave and hustled back inside. "Oh my gosh! I hope he doesn't come running over here."

Before walking beyond the brick wall, she turned to look back, and he shouted, "I'm callin' you tonight!"

She shouted back, "Cool!" Then, she rushed inside to see her mother standing in the middle of the floor with a huge you-met-a-cute-young-man smirk on her face.

"I see you made some friends already."

Dina glared at her mom with the heavy grocery bags dangling from her fingers feeling like she was caught doing something wrong when she wasn't doing anything wrong at all. Meanwhile, her mother escaped to the kitchen in her dingy night wear to unpack the groceries that she'd already brought inside. Sitting the bags down on the floor, she immediately turned around and shut the door only to double check the lock before looking through the peephole. Everything was clear. She breathed a sigh of relief and finally answered her mother as she took the bags into the kitchen.

"Yeah, when I went to the café around the block today, I met a guy named Michael who goes to the same school where I'll be going. He's a basketball player, but he used to run track."

"Really?"

"Yeah, he seems nice. We connect on sports, so we vibe."

"Vibe, huh?" her mom winked, making Dina slightly embarrassed once again.

"Mom, don't. I don't like him like that. We are friends, and that's it. Why are you so goofy?"

"If your dad was here, he would have..."

"Yeah, but he's not so," Dina interrupted, not in the mood for discussing what her father would or wouldn't have said and done because he was no longer around. She hadn't been able to talk about him since they buried him last year. Her mom would sometimes try and ease her into a conversation about him believing that Dina needed to release all of the grief she kept bottled away inside her heart, but Dina never wanted to do so. She only wanted to move on, out of fear of confronting it for what it really was.

"Well, I'll fill in for him," she concluded, turning to stack the canned products in the cabinet while taking the I-don't-want-to-talk-about-it hint Dina dropped heavily on the conversation. "Here's some salmon and sardines. Good and healthy meat to keep you from the hot dogs and salami that you somehow seem to find when I'm not around."

Dina laughed. "I can't put ketchup and mustard on my salmon, Ma. It doesn't work. It's more about the ketchup and mustard being on a specific meat. That's what does it for me. It's the combination of it all."

"Whatever you say." Her mom shook her head. "I'm just trying to keep you healthy, at least until you decide to leave me all by my lonesome."

"I won't ever leave you, Mom. I'll try my best to always call and come back and visit no matter where I am." She walked over and gave her mother a kiss on the cheek.

"And go brush your teeth."

"Oops! I forgot! I was asleep, wasn't I?" Dina said putting her hand over her mouth while walking to the bathroom to brush her teeth. She held her hand out in front of her mouth and blew her breath onto it to find out how bad it smelled. "Oh my gosh. You're right," she laughed.

"Dinner will be up soon. I'm not watching anything tonight. I'm fairly tired so I will take my food in the bedroom along with that salad and pie you bought for me, and you can have the television all to yourself."

Dina shouted back, "Okay!"

Dinner was complete in no time. Dina's mom made the spaghetti while Dina finished cleaning up in the living room and dining area, breaking down the boxes and running them outside to the dump in order to make their new home more cozy. Having the floors all swept and ready to eat was a treat. She convinced her mom to stay in the living room for a little bit before going to bed. Grace did, and they laughed at a comedy before Grace got up with her plate, kissed her daughter on the cheek goodnight and headed to bed. It wasn't soon after that Dina finished her food, raked her plate out, and washed it that the telephone rang.

"Hello?" It was almost ten p.m.

"Hi, this is Michael. May I speak to Dina, please?"

She took the phone from her mouth, spun around and fell onto the sofa with a newfound burst of energy because she knew exactly who it was. She had been eagerly waiting the call. "You thought I was my mother," she giggled.

"No, nothing like that. I just don't know your voice too well yet, and I didn't want to be disrespectful. First impressions, you know?"

"You plan on sticking around that long to care about a first impression?"

"Friends stick around, right?"

"Oh...yeah...friends."

He laughed at her pause between words. "I don't know if you're feelin' me like that, so I have to flex a little bit before I seal the deal."

"I saw your flex earlier," Dina smiled, as she twirled the curls in her fro.

"Oh that little thing," he replied.

"Yeah, that little thing." Then there was an awkward silence. "You have no idea what thing, do you?" Dina laughed quietly to not disturb her mother.

"You're right. I was over here trying to figure out what I did so I can do it again."

"Conversation. I liked it. I've always been a sucker for conversation."

"Meaning you're attracted to conversation."

"Basically," she sang, enjoying the moment of putting him on the spot.

"Well, I better keep talkin' good before you ghost me," he sighed, feeling really good and relieved about how things were going between himself and Dina.

"You better. But can you tell me something?"

"What?"

"You didn't..." Just then there was a knock at the door. "Mike, hold on, okay? I think these kids are playing around at the door again. They've been doing it since we moved in here." She put the phone down and went to the window instead of the door to see if she could catch who it was knocking and running. When she didn't see anyone at the window, she checked the door, deciding against the peephole based on what happened earlier. Cracking the door, she didn't see anyone, so she shut it back and grabbed the phone. "Yeah, I'm back."

"Everything alright?"

"Yeah, just some kids..."

"Kids?"

"Yeah."

"You sure?"

"Yeah, why?"

"I mean, I don't know *everything* about my community, but no kids live or hang over there at all. They normally roam on the next two blocks, not over there. Plus, all that aside, it's a bit late, don't you think, for kids to be out playing? Did you see them?"

"Well, no, but what do you mean no kids live or hang around here?"

"It's just not where they want to be is all."

Dina wondered about what he said and then replied, "And why would they not want to be around here in this area? They way you said it makes it seem like something is wrong."

"Nah, it's just superstition. You know how people make stuff up."

Dina didn't believe him. She could sense he wasn't being completely honest. "No." She straightened herself up on the chair, far more serious than the whimsical conversation just seconds ago. "No, I don't know how kids make stuff up. Why don't you tell me?"she asked, recalling how he reacted after finding out where she lived.

"Ahh, man, Dina," he complained.

"Ahh, man, Mike," she mocked him. "If it's something everyone else knows around here, I wanna know, too. I'm a new resident here, me and my mom, so don't you think I need to be informed, and then let us decide if it's superstition or not? It's not like there's a neighborhood paper or something."

"Actually, there is. It's run by Mr. & Mrs. Clance," he explained. "They put one out online. You can pick up printouts from them, too."

Dina's mouth dropped in disbelief. "We actually have a neighborhood bulletin, like a school newspaper?"

"Yeah, it sounds corny, huh? It's cool though. Some of the stuff they put in there is alright. I can't lie. I've stopped by and picked one up from time to time. I think they do it to keep busy. They're older and retired."

"What's inside, just jobs and stuff?"

"What went on in the neighborhood throughout the week, vacancies, what new stores are opening and coming around us, and it even has a whole list of the school sports schedule. It's not bad."

"Does it talk about what I asked you about?" Dina asked, sensing that he was relieved to get off the subject, therefore, she brought it back around in hopes that the tension would be down.

"About?"

"The kids. Why don't they play around here?"

"Their parents want them to stay close. It uh," he paused. "Some superstitious stuff from a long time ago that's all. Not a big deal, like I said."

Dina stood up from the sofa and paced around a bit before going back to the window. There was a light breeze playing with the leaves of the trees while shoving a piece of white paper down the sidewalk. She patiently waited before becoming impatient with Michael dodging what needed to be said. "Something like what, Mr. Not a Big Deal?"

"Some people went missing," he said quietly, wanting to change the subject. "But yeah, it's just superstition now."

"What's the superstition, and how does it go?" Dina stared into the nightfall as she sat on the window sill listening to Michael breathe until he responded.

"It's a rhyme the parents made up to make the children stay close to home. It's not really real, but..."

"Mike," she paused, highly irritated. "For real."

"Stay away from that place, that place over 'dey. Stay, just stay, close to home so you won't end up gone, long gone," he sang, singing it in the dialect it which it was created by the older folks of the community.

Dina stood up from the window sill. "That's it?" she said disappointed. "That's something regular. It's like saying don't talk to strangers."

"It works. Kids don't go over there, so I know for a fact it wasn't kids that knocked at your door."

"None?"

"None."

Dina slowly walked back over to her front door, and as she did, Michael was busy changing the subject. She hoped that there would be another knock on the door so that she could prove Michael wrong. However, there wasn't. The longer she was on the phone with him and no one knocked, the more paranoid she got. If it wasn't children knocking, then who was it?

"Mike, can I call you back tomorrow?" she asked, cutting him off slightly frustrated because the situation had reached a higher level of irritation due to the assumption that it wasn't little children, but teens or adults who were knocking at her door playing jokes.

"Of course you can."

"Yeah."

"It's my mom. She has to use it, so..." she lied.

"Oh, you don't have a cell phone?"

"We sort of can't afford one right now. I have to wait at least two months so my mom can rearrange the bills and make sure the money is going where it should. She doesn't want me to find a job and help out because she really is trying to keep me focused on getting into college.

She actually told me to wait until I get into college to get a job because I can schedule better."

"Okay, well make sure I talk to you tomorrow. Can we meet up?"

"Yeah. We'll meet up. Gotta go." She hung up the telephone. "Lord, forgive me for lying, but," she paused, sneaking to the door, "I just don't understand this, all the noise." Then, she finally had an idea on where the knocks and thumps could have been coming from - the lump in the floor. She leaned down to touch it. They'd been walking over it since they moved in, but didn't think much of it. "Is it the plumbing?"

Quickly, she remembered where she was when she heard the first knocks, and it was when she was in the kitchen pouring a glass of water. That sent her into the kitchen to run the water through the pipes. She turned on the water and then even wondered if her mother had also gone into the master bathroom and turned on the water while she was on the phone with Mike.

"That was probably it. The pipes," she said to herself as she eased back out of the kitchen, awaiting the knocking noise. She moved over to the hump in the floor, placed her ear down to it and waited.

The water flowed through the faucet, and everything was quiet. She heard nothing in the floor, so she stood up and went back to turn the water off. Feeling silly, she shrugged her shoulders and told herself to get over it until it happened again.

Nearly tripping over herself to get to the front door, she looked out of the peephole. She saw no one, so she turned on the outside light. She saw no shadows hiding out beside the door or anything, but just as she flicked the light off, the outside light from the condo across from hers came on.

"What?" Her eyes dropped to the huge realtor lock on the door. It had been locked since they moved in and still was. There was no way anyone was inside...unless they'd broken in. "Hey, mom!" she called. "Mom!" She called a couple more times until her mom dragged herself down the hallway, slightly irritated, but ready to address whatever problem Dina was having.

"What is it, baby. What's wrong? Is someone at the door?" she asked, rubbing her bloodshot eyes. It was obvious she was extremely tired.

"Ma, somebody's in there, the home across from us, but not in a legit way. They broke in," she whispered, "The outside light just came on, but the lock is still on. Look! Should we call the police? What if they come over here?"

"Scoot out of the way, Dina, and stop whispering. Let me see," her mom ordered firmly as she rolled her eyes and looked out the peephole. "Dina, are you sure the light was on?"

"Wait, what?" Dina asked confused. "I just moved from the peephole, and it was on. I was literally on, Ma. I wouldn't wake you up for nothing."

Grace turned from the door, put both her hands on her daughter's shoulders and stared her directly in the eyes. "I'm going back to bed. If you actually see burglars, call the cops. If you don't, just come to bed. Put some stuff up to the front door just in case, but I don't think anyone is in there."

"But..."

"Dina, think about it. The place is empty. Steal what?" She backed away from Dina, put her hands in the air and then walked around her. "Maybe the light was a glitch in the wiring, baby. Goodnight." She headed back to her bedroom and shut the door.

Dina couldn't believe it. She immediately went back to the peephole, and the light was off until it flicked back on. The light was even brighter this time, like someone changed the bulb within in seconds. Dina pulled her face back and readjusted, but when she went back to the peephole, to her astonishment, there were the same people she saw before.

The man was pacing back and forth, but his face didn't display the carefree, jovial smile that was there the first time Dina saw him.

Instead, his smile had dimmed to nothing, and his movements were as if he'd lost something so dear. He hung his head low, tracking the floor until halting, forcefully pointed to the other side of the room, and then stormed over to the area.

Dina tried to follow him to where he went but he was out of her field of vision. She backed away. Her mouth became as dry as an arid desert, and when she swallowed, there was nothing but air that cascaded down her throat. She was tempted to call her mother, but she didn't. Instead, she opened the front door in all skepticism, and just like before, no one was there. She then slammed it shut.

"Dina!" her mom shouted from the bedroom, obviously awakened by the slamming of the front door.

"I'm fine, Ma. Sorry," she stuttered, realizing that her mother was very frustrated at that point.

Dina was shaken up. She didn't know if something was wrong with her or if what she was seeing was true. Why was it that her mother didn't ever see or hear what she saw or heard since they moved into the condo?

At that point, Dina started to question her own sanity. She went and sat on the sofa, mentally drained and completely on edge before becoming discouraged. "What's wrong with me?" Tears welled up in her eyes, and she began to rock back and forth, thinking about her future endeavors and what seeing all those odd hallucinations meant. Obviously, they couldn't have been real, but they seemed to be because she wasn't asleep. She was really seeing it with her own eyes. Quickly glancing back up at the peephole while wiping the tears from her eyes, she whispered, "But I'm only seeing it when I stand at the door."

CHAPTER 3

"Are you alright? What are you doing up so early, and your eyes look like you got less sleep than me and you normally sleep like a log? Bloodshot eyes and everything."

Dina continued to look down into her bowl of cereal, not really wanting to answer anything. She knew she couldn't ignore her mother though because that would be disrespectful and bring on worse problems. "I'm alright. I had... I couldn't sleep." She was still hesitant to tell her mother what she saw last night because the last thing she wanted to do was concern her about visions or her mental health. It was highly possible that she was going through some sort of psychotic episode, but to tell her mother would be to put stress on her, more than necessary, and she didn't want to do that. Most of all, she didn't want to accept it herself.

All night long, Dina wanted to use the internet, but she wasn't able to because of the wait her mom put on the bills that weren't necessities. What she decided to do, however, was find out where the library was located and look some information up pertaining to what was going on with her mentally. She felt fine, but she didn't know if she was coming down with whatever mental break down her father had that contributed to his death.

"Mom, I'm gonna find the library today. I need some books to read, and uh…" she drifted. Her mom noticed the hesitancy in Dina's demeanor, as if something was wrong, so she sat down with her to eat before heading out to work.

"The library to find some books, huh, over the summer? This is a first for you. You're normally engulfed in music when you aren't practicing track, but I guess since the keyboard hasn't been delivered yet…" she probed but didn't get a reaction from Dina, so she continued. "I don't know where the library is, and you don't have a phone so I want you to stay close. If it's too far, and I mean more than a couple blocks out of this neighborhood, no. I haven't made my rounds yet."

"Can I ask Michael? He walked me back to house safe, and he's basically a classmate. I won't be anywhere with him but the library if it's not too far out."

"When I get to work, I'll ask a couple people where it is so that I know your location for my own sanity." She then thought about Dina's request, sighed and then responded, "I don't care if you ask Michael. I saw him from the window, so I know what he looks like down to his sneakers," she paused. "Are you sure you're okay?"

"Just sleepy. I'm gonna try to take a nap before I go."

Her mom nodded and continued to eat her instant oatmeal quickly before heading off to work, reminding Dina to keep the place secure. "Write down Michael's full name, too, and his phone number. Leave it right here on the table, plus what you're gonna be wearing."

"Mom, really?" Dina groaned, but didn't complain too much because her mother was just trying to give her what she called *careful* space not *dangerous* space in her teenage years.

"Yeah, really. In case something happens, I can describe what you were wearing. We've been doing that since forever, so don't behave like I'm going to stop now that you're nearly eighteen years old. Love you. Bye. And let him know that I know everything, and that if he harms you, they are coming for him because I know who you're with. It's a no win. Don't forget to write down his license tag number, too."

"Mom!" Dina strained, completely overwhelmed with all her instructions.

"Love you. And come straight back. Don't stay gone too long. Pick up the phone when I call. That means you should be back at four o'clock to answer my call or I know something is wrong."

"Mom," Dina groaned in an even lower tone. "Love you, too." She lifted her eyes as her mother fled like she knew she was about to be stuck in morning traffic. Dina looked at the wall clock that continued to sit on the floor because they had no nails to hang it. She sure was about to be late. "Drive safe!" she shouted instead of walking to the front door. She didn't want to approach the peephole at all until she felt better about it.

Although she wanted to call Michael, she didn't call him because it was much too early in the morning to call anyone's home, especially about going to the library of all places. She decided that she wasn't going to bother with asking him to go with her at all. Once he found out why she was going, he would probably think she was losing her mind, so she decided to walk down to the café because it opened at seven thirty in the morning. She could then ask them for directions to the closest library.

As she dressed, she noticed the brightness of the morning change. She walked to the window to inspect the weather as she put on her black and white sneakers. It was just as she suspected. It was going to rain, but it looked like the rainfall wouldn't be that heavy, therefore, she packed a couple of apples in her book bag along with a three lunch box drinks and headed out the door without looking up until she was beyond the peephole.

As soon as she stepped onto the sidewalk, minute droplets of moisture spread across her face. There was a light mist which made her hair smile. The street was busy, but the sidewalk was clear, that was until she turned the corner. Loads of people lined up at the café. There were so many people that the line was outside. She paused for a moment, figuring it may not have been the best time to hassle someone about the location of a library.

As she turned back to go home, having decided to possibly call Michael later, she recalled what he said about the Clances and how they created a news bulletin about what's going on in the neighborhood.

"Excuse me," she quickly stated, stopping someone who was passing by her. "The Clances for the paper? Do you know where I can find them or the paper?"

The older gentleman nodded his head with a mouth full of what looked to be a bagel that he'd partially bitten before stating, "Oh, yeah, yeah yeah, go straight," he swallowed, cleaning out the corners of his mouth with his tongue before continuing again, "And it will be the corner condo with an orange sign on it. Can't miss it. It will read Clances. Papers should be right there on the stoop." He walked off rapidly, limping, but still moving fast.

"Thank you!" She then headed off, wondering if she should have just asked him where the library was in the first place. However, it was too late. "I probably wouldn't have been able to remember how to get there anyway if it's too far."

As she walked down the street, she stumbled upon exactly what she was looking for – the Clances' home. There was a rather large, orange sign on the door, just like the man stated, and it read The Clances.

"Easy enough." Dina crossed the street and headed over, but as she scanned the stoop, there were no papers. "Figures." Then, she looked up. "There probably aren't any sitting out because of the rain." As she approached, having no idea why she felt so nervous, she began to rehearse a friendly greeting in her imagination.

She reached the door, and the aroma of a hardy breakfast filled her nose. It smelled like pancakes, stacks of them, with thin slices of bacon and scrambled eggs, much better than the cereal she ate that morning which left her hungry. Before she knocked, the door opened, and there stood a jovial, older lady wearing a red, checkered apron over a one piece dress with thick shoulder straps along with thick, orange slippers on her feet.

"Well, I saw you standing there and didn't know what was wrong with you. Come on in, and welcome to the neighborhood. Do you want something to eat? I'm hungry. You're the new one, you and your mother. Go ahead and sit down here."

"Mrs. Clance?" Dina asked, throwing her whole planned introduction to the side since Mrs. Clance hadn't let her say one full sentence yet.

"That's me," she said, leaning over the table to get an extra plate, picking the pancake up with her bare fingers and slapping it on a plate that Dina assumed was for her. Therefore, she walked over and slid into the chair, thanking her for the invite to breakfast.

"I'm Dina. I came over to ask about a newspaper."

"Like everybody else. They don't ever come in and sit down anymore like they used to do. Everybody is so busy now, including the children like you. Sports and this and that. You need to just sit and learn sometimes just how to sit, be still and listen. Watch for things. You'll be surprised."

"Surprised?"

"Let's eat." She plopped down and started slicing her pancakes. "It's been so long since I had someone your age in here. You bring an energy that I can't explain. God knew what He was talking about when he said reproduce. My child has been gone a while now. I miss him all the time. He used to sit right there where you are now, but he filled in the seat. He was a big one. Died from stepping out in the street too fast. I always told him to think before he acts. He was that kind though, similar to you all now. Go, go, go! Went too fast that time. That car killed my baby. My other child I lost when she was a baby. So I had two, but one I learned, and the other only learned me. You got no siblings, do you?" She stopped talking and stared at Dina strangely. "Aren't you gonna pick up your fork and eat?"

"Oh, yes ma'am." Dina grabbed the fork and shoved two pieces of pancakes in her mouth. She could feel her cheeks poking out, and it was difficult for her to control it, but she put a napkin up to her mouth to hide the fact that her mouth was entirely too full.

"Well, I didn't say choke yourself. Take some of that out."

Dina did just that, but right afterward, answered her question. "No, no ma'am. I don't have any siblings. How do you know so much about me?"

"Well, I'm Mrs. Clance. I'm the journalist around here. What I see, I write about. It's just that easy. Got my degree in it and all. You see that diploma up there?" She turned her eyes toward the back wall. "I can write like nobody else and tell a tale like you wouldn't believe. That's why I know who you are. I'm always watching, and I'm always writing."

"Are you gonna write about me and my mom in the paper?"

"No. I won't write about you, but I will know about you. I'm a good kinda nosey...not the bad kind. You don't have to worry any."

"I came by, not just for a paper, but because I needed to know where the closest library is around here."

"Oh well that's easy. Follow the road on down past my place, then take a left, right and left as soon as the left, right and left come.

There's your library. It's right next to the elementary school. It closes up at six o'clock, so you have plenty time to finish that pancake."

"How much are the papers?"

"Donate. Just take one for free, and when you get some money, put it through the hole in my door. See that?"

Dina looked over and there was a hole in the door at the bottom. It was big enough to fit a half dollar in and any paper money. Glancing back at Mrs. Clance, Dina thought to ask about her husband. "Aren't you married?"

"He's back there...mad. He wanted some grits, and I wanted pancakes, so I told him to come and cook what he wants, and I'll cook what I want. I suppose he wants nothing now because that's what he's eating back there – nothing."

Dina started laughing as Mrs. Clance pierced her lips like she didn't care one way or the other if Mr. Clance didn't eat all day long. She was glad to have met Mrs. Clance who looked to be in her seventies, but she moved like she was in her fifties. She didn't miss a beat.

Obviously physically and mentally fit, the only way one would know her age is by the way her voice crackled when she spoke.

"Thank you, Mrs. Clance. I'm going to go now. I want to catch the library and get back home before a certain time. I'll put some money through your door when…"

"Don't tell me. Never tell me. I'll be looking for it if you tell me. Just do it. Surprise me. It's nothing like waking up in the morning to a floor full of money," she grinned and hit her thigh. "Any money that comes through, I can assume it's yours like I do with everyone."

"Well, thank you again." Dina saw the newspaper bulletins sitting at the side of the door, so she picked one up before heading out as Mrs. Clance followed her to the door. As Dina made it down the steps, Mrs. Clance called her name.

"Yes ma'am?"

Mrs. Clance's face wasn't as jovial as it was when she was inside the house. Instead, she was staring down at Dina like she'd seen a ghost. Then, she spoke.

"Are you getting along good over there in your new place?"

A bit shaken by the way Mrs. Clance's demeanor suddenly changed, Dina almost forgot to reply, but she spoke up, "Yes...ma'am." Mrs. Clance didn't say anything back, but that smile that Dina was greeted with earlier never returned to her face. Even as Dina attempted to lighten things by waving, Mrs. Clance didn't lift her hand to wave back. She stood there like a pillar of salt.

As Dina turned the corner, she felt Mrs. Clance's eyes on her until she was completely blocked by the building. "Goodness," she sighed as she slowed down a bit feeling a sense of relief. "That was weird. I won't go back in there any time soon. What the heck was that all about?" she said to herself as she rushed her way to the library. The sprinkling had already stopped, but the cloudy sky appeared like it was holding onto a heavier dose of water for later, and she didn't want to be caught in it.

   The library was exactly where Mrs. Clance said it would be, and that was a relief for Dina because at the end of their meeting, she felt like Mrs. Clance could have possibly lied, despite being a gracious and good cook. As Dina walked into the library, the coolness of the air hit her hard. She hated being too hot and too cool when indoors, and it looked like she was going to have to tough it out because the temperature in the library was cooler than her liking. Other than that, the place appeared to have been freshly renovated or either brand new. There was a freshly-cleaned, lemon scent that swept the atmosphere, and that was unlike any library she'd ever entered. All the libraries she'd ever entered smelled like old rugs with a hint of light paper dust in the air. This library, however, smelled like someone cared to spruce it up a bit or had grown a disdain for the book odor day in and day out.

The short, stocky woman at the front wearing a nice, lime green blouse greeted Dina with a smile as she entered, and Dina returned the greeting with a cordial nod. Immediately, she saw the sign that read non-fiction, and she moved in that direction. She didn't want to search via the computer first because she thought she may run into what she was searching for by scanning the shelves, but she didn't. Thus, she ended up at the computer anyway.

Feeling self conscious, she took a deep breath and searched schizophrenia and hallucinations. A sense of panic came over her because it was such a sensitive subject for her to think about, even apply to herself, because it was what doctors said drove her father to the point of death, to the point that he purposely put himself out there in front of that eighteen wheeler and died. Her mom and others maintained it was an accident for a long time, that he'd somehow crossed the road at the wrong time. However, his car wasn't broken down on the side of the road. It was actually still running and in park when the police arrived with the door still open. He wasn't even hit while standing on the side of the road. He was hit in the middle of it. He'd walked over there. Dina never wanted to talk about it. His mental and psychological changes came on suddenly, and she was afraid that the same thing was happening to her.

She found some books specifically on the topic of mental illness, and as soon as she turned around to go locate them on the shelf, a librarian stopped her.

"Hello," she greeted with a smile. "If you're in need of any assistance, I'm here. Just let me know. I didn't mean to startle you," she continued, aware by how Dina seemed to be flustered by her presence.

"Oh, no thank you. I think I can manage. I saw the non-fiction sign as soon as I entered."

"There is also another non-fiction section upstairs."

"Upstairs?"

"Yes. This non-fiction section is for young adults and the other section, which is upstairs, is for adult reading, topics that go more in depth, so depending on the subject matter, it's good to know where you can find both," she explained, already peeping at the computer search behind Dina who forgot to clear it out. The librarian stood there with an odd smile on her face. She was extremely short, with a blonde, loosely curled cut atop her round, chubby face. Her lipstick was smeared, wiped upward toward her cheek, like she'd just finished eating something and wiped instead of dabbed. When the librarian continued to stand there, Dina responded with a nod, located the staircase, and bolted to it, relieved to be away from the librarian as she made her way up. She knew it was her own paranoia that made her feel so self conscious, but she couldn't fight the feeling of being on edge. Strangely, she had a sick sense that everyone knew what she was going though, like she was already being pointed out as the different one.

The staircase was large and winding with a break midway up. From the breaking point, Dina saw only two others who were seated, already researching and taking notes. They looked like college students.

She'd memorized the location of the book, so it wasn't going to be too hard for her to find. As she walked down the aisle, she placed her index finger on the book spines until she landed on the book she wanted. Quickly, she pulled it out, found an empty table in the corner away from everyone else, and began to read about schizophrenia first and then hallucinations. Reading the words took her back to her first times secretly researching about her father, and as she read, her eyes began to tear up. The words ran together, and she was forced to shut the book.

Trying to pull herself together, her throat pained as she forced her agony back. She began to frantically search for a bathroom, and when she saw the women's room, she quickly went inside, locked the door and cried. She gripped the doorknob tightly, fighting the memories of her father that she continuously found ways to escape, until she became overwhelmed by her thoughts of him and sank to the floor.

"Daddy," she wept, wishing she had him back in her life and not understanding anything about what went through his head or heart the day he died. "Please come back and help me. What's wrong with me? I don't wanna die, daddy. What's wrong with me?" she continued to ask him, fearful of her hallucinations leading her down the same path as he, but he never answered. He simply was not there anymore, just that easy and just that suddenly.

Finally, Dina became angered as she always had since his death whenever she had to confront her heartache. She hated all of what it felt like because it was never ending. There was a void in her heart that she couldn't fill, and it continued to grow. Time was supposed to make it better, but for Dina, it was only making it worse.

She got up from the floor, walked to the sink and washed her hands before wiping her face off. Her eyes were already bloodshot from crying for such a short time, and she hated for anyone to see her broken, therefore, she remained hidden until all traces of despair disappeared. When she exited, she walked beyond the area where she was seated, descended the staircase and left the library to enter beneath the pouring rain. She didn't rush home. Instead, she pondered over her mental state and the mental state of her father when he committed suicide, all the while, drowning under the rain, strolling in sorrow.

When she arrived home, instead of ignoring the condo across from her home, she decided to face it. She was soaked from head to toe, and as she stood there drawing absurd conclusions from strange occurrences that didn't make sense since she moved in, the rain water fell from her clothes, causing a small puddle around her feet. Breathing slowly, she glanced down at the realtor's lock on the door, and then she glanced at the peephole to cautiously look inside...until she was interrupted.

"I thought that was you."

Dina jumped back from the peephole to see Michael approaching to her left. Quickly, she looked down, unsure of what she looked like after becoming so upset, and atop that, soaked. Then, she moved away from the door and headed to her own.

"Hey, Mike," she responded, camouflaging how she felt on the inside by sounding up beat. "What are you doing over here?"

Mike stood there for a second, debating on whether or not he should go off his impulse and joke about her peeping through the peephole of the other door or letting it go. He felt something was wrong, but he couldn't put his finger on it. He just felt it.

"What's up?" he hesitated, as he moved towards her, also glancing at the other door. "I saw you as I was driving by. Why are you out here walking in the pouring rain?"

"I got stuck in it actually," she said as she opened her front door and walked inside. He noticed how she failed to look him in his face at all, leading him to believe that she may not have even wanted him there. He didn't enter the home, but stopped at the entrance.

"Next time, you can call me. Maybe I can give you a lift where you have to go. Most times, I'm up early exercising anyway, so..."

"Yeah, I didn't think about that, you know, disturbing you so early. I don't wanna be that type of ..."

"Type of what?" he cut her off as he continued to stand outside the door. She turned around.

"Oh, you can come inside, Mike. I didn't mean for you to stand out there like that. That's why I left the door open behind me."

"Yeah, but I don't walk inside anybody's place without being invited, but now that I am invited," he responded, sliding inside and closing the door behind him. "Calling me would have been fine. Remember, we were supposed to meet up today some time anyway."

"Right. I forgot about that. Do you mind? I have to go change up. Have a seat. Sorry about the mess, but we haven't quite finished cleaning up and unboxing things."

"No problem. Sure, go ahead. I know what it's like," he responded, sitting down on the sofa, taking a look at a small, framed picture of Dina and who he assumed to be her mother and father. "So is this your mother? You and her look just alike, but wait, I'm sure this is your dad because you have many of his features, too."

"Yeah," she called from her bedroom. "That's mom...and uh..." she continued as she walked from the room with dry clothes on. "Yeah, that's dad. He's gone," she stated, not wanting to mention anything else about him because his death was all over the news the day he passed away. The suicide shut down traffic on the whole highway. Her father's picture and name were plastered on the news. Many people knew him since he was an activist in the community, and lots of people knew him in the neighboring cities before he lost his mind because he would travel constantly.

"I'm sorry to hear that. He looks familiar, like I'd seen him before somewhere."

Dina pretended like she didn't hear him, and went into the kitchen to get some drinks. "Want something to take down?"

"Yeah, what ya' got?"

"Just some juices. Grape or cherry?"

"Grape."

She walked from the kitchen with the juices in her hand along with a bowl of grapes and raspberries. "I hope you don't mind, I'm hungry. There's enough for you in the bowl, too, so feel free." She then sat beside him on the couch.

"Thanks." He took the drink and tried to relax, but it still felt like either he wasn't really welcome or something was wrong. Sitting at the edge of the sofa, he started, "Dina, I can leave, you know. I just was checking you out since I saw you. You're giving me some vibes like you're upset, and I know we just met, but those vibes are strong. Are you alright?"

Dina put her head down. She didn't have an extra excuse to give him, but she was sure she wasn't hiding how she felt as well as she thought she was. "No, you're fine. You aren't imagining things either," she said as she reached over and turned the framed picture of her family face down. "My father was the one who died on the highway. That's how you know him," she sighed, "or you may know him as an activist who had been on television from time to time fighting for justice, but that was years before he died."

Michael didn't know what to say, but he did know who he was after Dina triggered his memory. "Dina, I'm sorry if I brought something up…"

"You didn't," she said, walking toward the window. "I was already upset. He didn't just die." She faced him. "He got hit by a truck. It wasn't an accident. It was suicide. He'd gone crazy or something. After all his life being sane, he suddenly went insane, and that was what happened."

"Hey, Dina," he said, standing to his feet and walking over to her when he saw tears in her eyes. "I'm sorry I brought it up. I didn't know." He went to embrace her, and she accepted the embrace. She hadn't accepted one in a long time when it pertained to her father.

"Truth be told, that was why I ended up walking in the rain."

"How about this?" He backed away slightly, having thought of something to lighten the mood. "Wanna go with me somewhere fun? The rain has slowed, and I'm buyin'."

"Well, let's go!" Dina exclaimed, glad that he wasn't pushing it and that he was on her team when it came to feeling good. She didn't want to dwell on it, and she was so glad she had someone to hang out with to take her mind off of everything that she felt she needed to forget. "Where?"

"Do you skate?"

"Do I?" she responded matter of factly.

"Well, let's go then." He looked back at the food. "We will get some lunch when we hit the rink. It should be open in thirty minutes. That's how long it will take us to get there."

"Lemme get my socks!" Dina ran off down the hall.

"I'll meet you outside."

"Okay!"she hollered back. "Let me redo my hair, too. It's not looking good up there," she laughed. Inside her bedroom, she was ecstatic. It was a relief to be able to hang out with Mike, and she would do anything to rid herself of the funk she was thrown in of her own making. "There's nothing wrong with me," she sighed as she gathered her hair back into a fresh fro to sit atop her head, put on a little lip gloss, and grabbed some socks before checking herself in the bathroom mirror. Suddenly, the front door slammed, startling her. "Mike?" she called, peeping out from the bathroom, believing that he'd re-entered. Then, she stepped out into the hallway. "Mike?" He wasn't there.

Quickly, she retreated to her mother's room and looked out the window. There was Mike. He hadn't re-entered. He was waiting on her right there on the street like he said he would. She turned and grabbed one of her mom's high heel shoes as a weapon before walking back down the short corridor. As she reached the living room, no one was there, but then she heard a strange laughter. It was coming from the front door.

"I knew it!" She raced to open the front door, but when she did, the giggling and laughter completely stopped. It was like whoever was there laughing, disappeared instantly. Dina shut the door quickly and made her way over to grab her keys when, suddenly, the giggling eerily resumed.

The denial, she put both hands over her ears and scooted away from the window in order to conceal her actions from Michael who may have caught a glimpse of her through the window. Leaning up against the wall, she took some deep breaths and closed her eyes in an attempt to calm her nerves and mental state, but the laughing didn't stop. Then came the noise, the thumps against the door, causing her to squeeze her eyes tighter until after a couple of seconds, it stopped. Everything stopped. Dina slowly dropped her hands from her ears and opened her eyes. Inhaling slowly, she convinced herself that she was just in need of a little fun, so she started on her way out when she heard the voice of a child call.

"Come here. Please, come here."

Dina spun around, darting her eyes everywhere because it sounded like the child was inside the home, possibly hiding. "Hello?" Dina called.

"Come over here," called the voice once again, causing Dina to accurately pinpoint the location of the voice. It was the front door again. Instead of bidding to the call, she fled, rushing the door like the track star she always dreamed of becoming, and left. The voice stopped when she was completely outside with the door locked.

Her adrenaline was heightened to a point that was nearly uncontrollable. Therefore, she took the time to calm herself. She really liked Michael and wanted the school year to start without a whole summer of rumors about her seeing and hearing things that weren't actually there.

Walking down the steps, she faked everything from her walk, to her confidence and smile. She was a complete wreck inside. There was Michael standing there watching her as she approached, and she dismissed everything that had just happened to her, creating some sort of outer body experience so that she could have a great time and bond with someone that she not only thought to be cute but a close new friend, hopefully a boyfriend.

"You ready to go?" she sang as she hopped down onto the sidewalk.

"Waitin' on you, Dina, baby," he responded.

"Oh, I'm baby now?" she responded as he held the car door open for her. "And I see somebody is doing the most for a little day at the rink." She sat down impressed at the attention and respect he was giving her.

He shut the door and leaned over into the passenger's side window as Dina situated herself in his car which smelled like he just had the interior cleaned. "If you ride with me, you don't have to worry about another female sittin' there, you know?"

She looked up. "What's that supposed to mean? That has several connotations, don't you think?" she giggled.

"No. It just has one," he responded, tapping the car before walking around to the driver's side leaving Dina there to wonder more about him as she watched him enter the car. "I know you know I like you, don't you?"

"Do you?"

"Stop playin'." He backed up the car. "Let me know after hanging out with me for a while if you're feelin' me, too. Deal?"

Dina could barely look at him without feeling giddy inside. Michael was fine, extremely fine, every time he looked at her, she melted internally but refused to let it show externally. Her mom taught her a couple years ago, after finding out she had a secret boyfriend, to always remain in control of herself. She said '*attraction can be sweet, but the last thing you want is a cavity, so control how much you take because it makes all the difference in the world. Keep your teeth.*'

"Yeah," she said, taking a deep breath as she got butterflies in her stomach. "I'll let you know."

"Alright." He put the car in gear and started down the street just as Dina remembered that she failed to leave the information for her mother about Michael. She didn't tell him to stop, however. She felt that he was being honest, and she would make certain she was back before her mom called.

As he drove, Michael talked about various things, mostly pertaining to the school and about his friends. When asked about his family,

Michael went in depth with that, too. Dina enjoyed asking him questions. She wanted to hear what he had to say. It also gave her an excuse to look at him, take him all in. His muscles bulged through his skin each time he turned the wheel, and the scar right beneath his chin made her wonder more about who he was and how it happened. Dina was caught up in an infatuation. She had a whole sweet tooth and was trying not to catch a cavity.

Pulling up to the rink, the place looked deserted. There were hardly any cars.

"Are you sure it's open?"

"Yeah, it's open. Normally, the place is empty until Saturday night. We're early, but they're open. It's summertime." He walked over to her door that she'd already opened and held the door as she exited. "It might just be me and you on the floor. What you think?"

"Less embarrassment for you," she bragged as she walked ahead of him.

"Okay, okay. I'm up for a little competition from the losing side. The only way you get better is by going up against the best. Ever heard that knowledge before?"

"And who might that best be?" she turned around, jumping up to look over his shoulder, behaving as if she was missing someone standing behind him.

"I see you got jokes. Come on and let me make one of you."

"Make a joke of me? Man..." Dina joked minutes before they were on the rink skating.

"You're a tower now," Dina stated at his height, commenting on his height while in skates as they made their way the smooth floor of the rink.

"Tell me about it. And this tower is about to show you how it's done!" he exclaimed as he took off, leaving her behind as he started to perform highly impressive tricks on his skates that Dina couldn't compete with at all. She didn't even try as he came back and grabbed her by the hands, pulling her along with him down the rink.

She was having a blast, and all that happened earlier in the rain and at her home was gone, as if it had never happened. Dina enjoyed his touch and how they both laughed and had fun all across the rink. He took her from behind, around her waist, and as the music changed, they skated to the beat until it stopped. They didn't speak. They didn't have to because the touch and silence spoke volumes about how much they liked each other.

They sat down at the concession to eat. As Michael walked over to buy some hot dogs and fries, she removed her skates. There was some community sanitizer in various spots in the rink so she walked over to clean off her hands before making her way back over to the booth. Michael was on his way back with the trays, so she made a detour to get the drinks from the counter before making it back over to sit and eat.

"The fries are hot," Dina stated, watching the steam from them as Michael watched her. She literally felt his eyes, so she decided to break his entertainment with conversation about it. "I see you staring at me, you know."

"I want you to see me." He sat up straighter in his seat before taking a bite of his hotdog. "You don't wanna see me?"

Dina felt embarrassed. She wasn't as confident as she thought she would be on the date, and she couldn't help but blush. "Stop, Mike," she smiled. "I'm trying to eat right now." She took a deep breath and bit on her fries.

"I'm trying to watch."

"Come on, Mike," she stressed as she put her fries down, folded her arms and laughed. "You're making me feel weird."

"Alright. I didn't know you were so shy," he said as he laid off. "Out there, you were talkin' big."

"That's only about sports."

"But not about me."

"No, not about you. Sometimes, you make me feel kinda..."

"Nice."

She finally looked back into his eyes. "Yeah, nice."

"You make me feel the same way."

"Well, it looks like you handle it better, Mike," she laughed and rolled her eyes. Then, she thought about her mother... and cavities.

"So are you telling me how you feel about me, or am I reading you wrong?"

"You're reading me right."

At that point, they ate, talked about everything under the sun, and put back on their skates to enjoy the rink a bit more before heading home. They'd been out for a while, and she knew she was cutting it close, especially when they got stuck in traffic. The clock inside the car read three-thirty.

"My mom is gonna kill me if I'm not back at four o'clock like I said I would be."

"She will? What's the problem?"

"She doesn't know you."

"She knew we were hanging out today?"

"Remember that we'd planned to hang out today?" she asked and he nodded. "Yeah, well, I'd sort of let her know about that so she wouldn't be concerned. She knows who you are...kinda. I just have to be back in time for her phone call or she'll probably..."

"Have a hit out on me?"

"Don't worry," she laughed. "I'll protect you."

"Don't worry." He took her by the hand as he drove through the intersection. "I'll get you back in time."

"Thanks."

He didn't lie. She was back home five minutes before four o'clock. She exited the car and invited Michael inside as she ran into the house.

"Come on inside. My mom won't be here until about five-thirty, so..."

"Well, am I supposed to be here? I know I came in before, but I wasn't aware that your mom had certain rules. I want you to keep her rules. It's easier that way. I don't wanna break them so she can break me."

"No, it's not like that. Don't worry about it. Oops, there she is!" she said as the phone starting ringing. She picked it up. "Hi, Mom! Yeah...yeah. Mom? Would you like to meet Mike?" she asked, spinning around on her toes to see the look on Michael's face. He'd already put his face directly into the palm of his hand. "Okay, well, I'll tell him to come inside since you'll be home in a bit. His last name?" Dina asked loudly to get Michael's attention who then said DeMonte. "It's DeMonte. Michael DeMonte, and he's eighteen. We ended up at the skating rink today, after I went to the library. Alright. See you when you get home. Love you." She hung up and then slid over to where Michael was on the chair. "You can stay!"

"I heard you over there, selling me to your moms."

"I wouldn't call it selling you but more like making her comfortable with you versus not wanting me around you at all. She doesn't like people who tend to hide out."

"I'm not hiding out."

"I know, but from her perspective, if I've already hung out with you, she may want to know who you are. She likes to get a feel for people, and if she doesn't, I'm on lockdown."

"Lockdown?" he laughed.

"She will lock me down in the house because I'm being secretive. Basically, if I'm honest, she can handle it. She can't handle secrets and lies. She raised me like that."

"Better than me. I got popped whenever I told the truth or lied. It was a no win," he laughed. "But I don't mind meeting your mom if you want me to." He went quiet. "I had fun with you today. I skipped my game and everything."

"You had a game?"

"Yeah, me and the guys."

"Oh, I'm sorry!"

"No, it was my choice. There's always another man out there on the court to take my place." He took her hand into his. She moved over closer to him, and they shared their first kiss. However, when Dina thought about cavities again, she pulled back. Then, she heard a knock. She was about to stand to go see who was at the door, but when she noticed Michael wasn't fazed by the knock, she sat there silent. At that moment, the distinctive knock happened again, but louder.

"Mike?"

"Yeah? What's up?"

"Do you hear that...little noise?" she asked, not wanting to identify it for what it really was. It sounded off again, causing her to leave the couch and go to the bathroom.

"What noise?"

"I'll be back. I have to use the bathroom really quick."

She walked down the hallway, and as soon as she was out of Michael's sight, she turned back around, baffled as she stared back at the front door. She panicked because Michael still wasn't moving and the knocking was still going on and at a more rapid rate. He really didn't hear it. It was just her. It was all in her head.

Shoving the bathroom door open, she immediately dropped to the floor onto her knees. The noise wouldn't stop. The beating was so loud, louder than the knocks had ever been.

Finally, she couldn't take it anymore. She stood up fuming, fled the bathroom, and ran beyond a stunned Michael while viciously shouting at the front door, "Stop knocking on the door!"

"What the??" Michael shouted, leaping from the couch as he watched alarmed at how Dina spread herself against the door like she was its decor, like she wasn't in control of herself at all. The side of her face slammed against the front door like someone slammed it there for her, and her right eye plastered against the peephole. Her arms stretched up and out in a diagonal fashion, all the way through her fingertips as if she was stretching her way to the top two corners of the rectangular door. Her legs remained straight as an arrow all the way through to her feet. She was posed like a diver taking off from a diving board.

"Dina? Dina…" He stumbled over his own feet as he crossed the sofa completely dumbfounded by what he saw. "Dina. Hey, Dina…"

However, Dina, didn't hear his call. She was watching, her right eye viciously moving side to side, forced to watch what was going on inside the peephole in order to make the noise stop. She couldn't pull herself away. Something very powerful was holding her there.

Completely terrified at what was before him, Michael found another way out of the condo - the back window - choosing not to go out of the front window because it would look like he was breaking and entering. No one was at the back, so that was the route he took, but once his feet hit the grass, he turned back around to look inside. He couldn't see Dina fully. The only part of her body that he could see was her feet, and they were elevated off the floor as she continued to be pressed flush against the front door. He wasted no time getting out of there, confused and afraid, leaving Dina stuck, glaring wildly, through the peephole.

CHAPTER 4

"Daddy?" The little girl tugged on his pant leg. "Daddy?" she continued to shout, yanking on her father before the boy came over, her brother, and began pulling on the other leg. Their father wasn't moving. He just lay there asleep as if he wasn't even alive.

The children began to play on him like he was a slide, climbing up and rolling back down. They also played a game of chase by running around their father as he continued to zone out in the chair. A bottle of beer rolled from his lap and spilled onto the floor, and the little girl picked it up and looked at it before putting it to her mouth. As soon as she did, she spit it out and laughed. Then, her brother did the same, tasted it and spit it on what he thought was the floor, however, it wasn't. It was his father's leg, and his father wasn't truly asleep. He saw and felt it what his son did.

Immediately, the father got up, grabbed the boy from his feet, lifted and violently shook him as his sister screamed at the horrific sight of her brother's body being hurled back and forth. It was at that moment that the child's mother ran into the room, throwing her entire weight upon her husband's huge arm in order for him to let loose of her son. The little boy fell the short distance to the floor, stood up petrified and ran away, hand in hand with his sister as their father slammed their mother to the floor. As she scrambled to get up, he shoved his foot into her back as she wailed for help. He held it there for thirty seconds, then, he finally removed his foot and walked away.

Dina fell from the front door, screaming uncontrollably, landing on the floor and shoving herself backwards until she was in the hallway. Suddenly, she remembered that she wasn't alone.

"Mike!" she called, searching but unable to find him sitting on the couch. "Mike!" She stood to her feet, shaking and afraid, wanting to leave, but not able to because she felt not only confused, but stuck. It was then that her mother burst through the door, earlier than her scheduled time to be home. She'd heard Dina from the street screaming Michael's name.

"Dina! Dina, baby! What's wrong? Tell Mama baby. What's wrong?" She looked around. "Where's that boy? Did he hurt you? Dina, answer me." Dina stared back at her trembling, unable to explain anything, so Grace furiously shouted, "Dina, answer me!"

Instead of answering, Dina's attention wandered beyond her mother toward the front door which was left wide open. She couldn't ignore it, and her mother noticed, so she attempted to block her from staring at the door. "Dina, baby, look at me. I'm right here. Right here in front of you. Did he do something to you? I heard you screaming his name from outside. Is he here? Answer me, Dina!" she shouted, needing to call the authorities if someone did harm her. Finally, because Dina continued stare outside the door, trembling like someone was staring back at her, Grace went to shut the door, but Dina lunged forward, grabbing her mother by the ankle, nearly resulting in her mother nose diving to the floor.

"Dina!"

"No! Don't shut it," Dina cried. "Leave it alone, Ma. Leave it open." She got up and ran in front of the doorway as her mother looked on in shock, not able to piece any of what was happening into anything that made sense.

"Dina, what is going on? I'm shutting the door."

Dina threw her hands up in an attempt to stop her mother. "Mama, no. They're in there," she wept, straining to convince her mother of what seemed ridiculous but was all too real.

"Who is in where, baby?" her mother asked, truly trying to understand because she knew Dina to never be an easy weeper. The sight of her tears broke Grace, but she tried to remain strong as her daughter continued to break down before her very eyes over something invisible...reminding her of her deceased husband. "Dina, look at me, baby. I'm right here. Nobody is over there, sweetheart," she said, choking back tears, frightened for Dina's frame of mind.

"Mama, it's true. I know you don't believe me, but it's true. We can't close the door, Mama. It's gonna force me to look inside. It keeps knocking, and I can hear it. It's not fake. It's real. It pulled me...it sucked me...like it wanted me in there."

There was silence as Dina stood shaken like a reed in the wind. Her mom didn't know what else to say. Finally, she asked.

"Wanted you in where?"

"The peephole, Ma. In the peephole."

"Yes. Yes. We're here. Thank you, Dr. Norris."

Dina trembled all the way to the psychiatrist's home on short notice that evening. Grace refused to allow any more time to pass before her daughter was seen by the same doctor who examined her father. She was terrified, but at the same time, determined to save her daughter unlike she did her husband.

"Come on inside, come on. Go to the right and enter," Dr. Norris said through the speaker, directing them to his office to which they would enter through the side of this home. When they reached the door, it was already open, and they rushed inside.

White walls greeted them along with white furniture and floors. The only colors that splashed the area were the spines of the books that lined the bookshelves behind his white oak desk as he sat in a black t-shirt and light colored denim jeans. He stood as they came inside.

"Have a seat, please," he stated while inspecting Dina's demeanor as she sat quietly but uneasily. Grace went over, shook his hand and noticed that he'd already retrieved paperwork on her deceased husband. She shut her eyes and went to sit next to Dina on the couch.

"I came home, and she was like this. She was panicking, and she hasn't told me anything except she wanted the door, the front door, to stay open because of something in the peephole. Doctor, I just don't know…"

"Dina," he lifted his finger slightly and politely interrupted, but she didn't respond. She looked away, toward the exit, and held her head down. "Dina. Tell me what you saw. Tell me what happened."

"The door. It was the peephole, Dr. Norris. They were in the peephole."

"Who?"

"I don't know… and they wouldn't let me go."

"They wouldn't let you go where?"

"I'm not crazy." She finally released her tears once again but quickly wiped them from her face. "They pushed my whole body against the door so I could see."

"Who is they?"

"I don't know!" she shouted, banging her fist against the cushioned arm of the seat.

"Dina," her mom interjected, but the doctor lifted his hand politely insisting that everything was under control.

"Dina, your father..."

"I'm not him," she rapidly rebuked.

"I know you're not, but your father was a great man. However, he suffered from anxiety, among other things that were triggered later in his life. What I want to do is make certain that nothing has stressed you or..."

"Mom, I'm ready to go."

"Dr. Norris," Grace started, "We just moved into a new place, and..."

"And it's not fake!" Dina yelled. "Psychological stuff isn't tangible like this is. What happened to me isn't fake," she continued, glaring at the doctor and then her mother. "I just told him what happened, and he's calling it stress, Ma! Stress? Stress doesn't plaster me into a door!"

Her mother continued, "There was a boy there named…"

"And I told you already! He didn't do anything to me! Listen to me," she yelled, frustrated with everything, however, when they sat there to listen as she asked them to, she stormed from the office. She had nothing left to say. Crossing the lawn but unable to get inside the car, she stood there, understanding full well how she appeared because it was how her father looked. He looked mentally ill. Maybe he was mentally ill, but she felt she wasn't. She knew she wasn't. She knew what she saw. It was real. She felt it.

Her mother came around the corner. In her hand was a small bottle of pills. Dina turned away from her, ready to get into the car and go. As her mother unlocked the door, she quickly opened the door and climbed in.

"Dina, listen," her mother started in, but Dina wasn't in the mood.

"Ma, I don't want to hear what he has to say. He's gonna say I'm crazy." She looked down at the medicine that her mother sat inside the cup holder, snatched it and threw it out the passenger's side window as she shouted, "And I'm not mentally ill. What I saw was real, and he shouldn't just automatically think it's my father in me!"

"He didn't think that, but some things could be genetic."

"Do genes throw me up against the door, Ma?" Her mother didn't answer because she didn't know how. To her, it sounded like something out of a horror movie. "No. That's the answer, Ma. No. Genes don't do that. I had no control over myself," she continued, but after listening to what she said about not having any control over herself, she knew she sounded mentally ill again. Therefore, she reclined the seat, put her hands over her face and cried as her mother backed out of the driveway and drove home, praying for her only child.

With carry-out seafood in hand, Dina exited the car. Instead of walking to the front door, she waited on her mother. Her mom noticed. It was Dina who normally beat her to the door, however, this night was different.

"Come on, Dina. Let's go," she sighed as she made her way to the door. Dina followed, completely insecure about not only going inside but anywhere near the place where her problems began.

"Mom," Dina called. Her mom turned back around, but didn't say anything. "Please believe me. Somebody's in there. It's in there. They're in there."

"Dina, just follow me in the house, and no one is there. Stay behind me."

"Not inside the house. In the peephole."

Her mom took a deep breath, but instead of arguing or attempting to change her mind while they stood outside, she decided to pretend like she was on her side. "Okay, but I'm here with you now. Whatever you see, I will see, and we will fight it together. Deal?" Dina nodded, and her mother tried to change the subject. "Besides, my feet hurt. We can just eat and drift off to sleep wherever we sit. How about that?"

Dina walked toward her, and they both approached the front door together. Dina's mind swirled about what she'd seen, and there was no way that what happened wasn't real. Walking beyond the threshold to enter into the small foyer increased her level of anxiety. She steered clear of closing the door behind her, opting to leave it open. Then, she fled into the kitchen to put down the seafood platter meals on the counter. When her mother didn't hear the door close, she walked back out of her bedroom, removing her other shoe. The front door was wide open.

"Dina," she called firmly. Dina heard her, but she didn't answer. "It's late. Close and lock the door...now. I've had a long day, and I need to shower and cool down some. Please. Lock the door. We can't allow this to change our safety practices and what you should be doing." Grace didn't hear Dina respond which was completely disrespectful, so slightly annoyed, she walked back to the front to shut the door herself. "Dina."

"Ma'am?"

Her mother walked to the kitchen and leaned against the refrigerator exhausted, "I'm trying. Meet me halfway. I'm not asking you to come all the way to me. Just meet me halfway on this. What am I going to do, Dina? I have to go to work, and I need you to shut the door alone in here and be okay. Can and will you meet me halfway? I'm not saying that I understand, but I'm trying."

Dina nodded but didn't look her mother in the eyes. Instead, she pulled out the plates and started separating the food and making the drinks. "I'll be better tomorrow. I'll stay in my room to get some sleep after you leave for work."

"What's his phone number?"

"Mom, it wasn't him. It just happened. I'm sure you can find him but you'll be attacking him for nothing and get yourself in trouble. If he'd hurt me, I would have told you and the police."

"Where was he when all this happened?"

"He left. I mean, I didn't see him leave, but he did."

"How didn't you see him leave, Dina? Why would he leave if you were in distress?"

Frustrated at her mom for continuously trying to lay blame on Michael, she shouted, "Mom! You're not listening!" Three of the shrimp fell to the floor, and even though her mother felt like making a fuss about the wasted food, she didn't. She held her peace. "It happened like I told you. I thought I was having a mental breakdown, too, and that was why I went to the library. But mental illness...it doesn't do what happened to me. I was on the door, Ma. On the door...like a pancake to a frying pan watching a family get abused and nearly killed by some man!"

"Where were the people that you saw? I need you to think about it... in reality."

Dina slammed her hand against the kitchen counter, knocking the rest of her food over into the sink. "I *am* in reality!" she shouted, consumed with anger. She wasn't angry at her mother. She was angry because she couldn't explain what was happening in any way that made logical sense. Suddenly, she quieted and repeated herself, "I am in reality. Ma, I'm sorry about shouting but it wasn't at you. It was at the situation."

Dina walked beyond her mother, feeling horrible about how she behaved with the doctor and how she was behaving at home with her mother. She went to her bedroom, didn't close the door because she didn't want to add to the tension that was growing, laid on her bed and silently cried. She'd lost her appetite, and she had nothing to eat anyway because she'd ruined it when she knocked it into the sink. It wasn't ten minutes later that her mother walked down the hallway with a plate of food for her, sat it on her bed, kissed her on the cheek and retreated to her own bedroom. Her mother had given her half of her meal with some fruit on the side.

Immediately, Dina rose from the bed, went into her mother's bedroom along with the plate of food and ate with her. They both fell asleep, her mother's arm around her like she was still a little girl.

CHAPTER 5

Her mom had already left for work, and Dina sat inside her room, growing more and more furious as the day dragged along. She continued to glare at the telephone that she'd moved into her bedroom. It hadn't rung as she expected. After sitting and waiting for fifteen more minutes, she finally decided to call.

The phone rang, but then, the ring was shut off, sending her straight to voicemail. That only made Dina more persistent because she knew that he was ignoring her. She called again. The phone didn't go to the recipient's voicemail, however, it wasn't answered either. She hung up, but as soon as she did, her phone began to ring. She knew it was him.

She took a deep breath. "Hello?"

"Dina?"

"You continued to ignore my phone call, and you left me when I was in trouble," she attacked, clearly upset that he left her in her time of need.

"Dina, what was I supposed to do?" he asked before saying, "Come outside. I'm outside."

"I'll come around the side."

"The side? Why?"

She hung up the phone and jumped out of her bedroom window which was low to the ground. Dina was determined to not exit from the front door, so the window was her only option. When she came around the corner, he was looking the other way, assuming she would come out from the other side. "I'm right here," she said walking toward him. He appeared startled.

"What's up?" he asked. Instead of his normal confidence, he portrayed nervousness and uncertainty. Therefore, Dina stopped about four feet away from him.

"Don't let me scare you off again," she stated, rolling her eyes.

Immediately, he took offense. "Did you not see yourself? One minute, you're in the bathroom, and the next minute, you're trying to run through the door like a character on one of those old school cartoons instead of opening the thing and walking out like a normal person! I called you a couple times, but you didn't answer. Look at me, Dina. You see what I look like?" he said pointing to his skin. "You know what the hell I'm thinking in my head if I put my hands on you? So I left! I shouldn't have even taken a detour to come over here to see you right now, but since we're outside in the broad daylight..." he said looking around, making sure everyone saw him being innocent.

Quickly able to see things his way, she apologized, "I'm sorry, Mike."

"I've never been in trouble in my life, and I got stuff I want to live for. I was scared to death, and your mom knew I was there. I just knew she would send the cops to my house making me a suspect in some stuff I did nothing to bring about. And there goes my dream life, so don't come out here like I had nothing to lose or my parents didn't have anything to lose like you're the only one..."

"I said I'm sorry! There's no way I tried to put you in any dangerous situation. I understand, Mike. I just didn't think about it from your eyes is all," she stated, then lowered her voice. "I know what it looked like. I know exactly what it looked like. I can explain it, but then again, I can't." She stared back into his eyes as he shifted his stance, leaning against his car, clearly still uncomfortable despite being a good distance from her.

"I'm not crazy," she continued quietly. "That wasn't me. Something pushed me."

"It wasn't *me* that pushed you. I didn't touch you," he postured up, stressing that fact.

"I know. I told my mom that you didn't do anything to me."

"See, man, I have to go..." he said, walking back to the driver's side of his car. "My mom told me about this place."

"What?" Dina ran over to the driver's side of the car, and Mike backed away.

"Watch out, watch out. Don't walk up on me. Your mom already thinks something bad about me. I worked too hard on my image so that people see I'm a good person, and I won't let you or anybody else take it from me, so... Just know I wanna be somebody."

"And I want you to be somebody! I didn't mean for this to happen... and you already are somebody, Mike, just being born! Only God can take that from you!" she shouted, frustrated with everything that was spiraling out of control. "Just tell me what you're talking about with your mother and what she said."

"I'm not superstitious. But those kids you said you were hearing all the time. There may be more to that and all of this that happened to you is all I'm saying."

"What are you talking about?"

"Man, Dina, nobody has lived in these two condos for years." Then, he stressed, "This particular section for years."

"Years?"

"Yeah. Rumors, I don't know how true though, of some freakish stuff that must have happened and kept happening until they locked it up. It wasn't until recently they put your condo up for sale. Let me guess. Your mom got it for a better deal than what other people pay around here."

"How should I know? I don't know what everybody pays."

"Anyway," he sighed, taking a deep breath. "It has something to do with some people, or somebody, I don't know. Ask enough people, you get ten more stories than the first ten you got. To be honest, I laughed at the stories half the time because they sounded like superstition or rumors because the stories kept changing, like some old tales. I still stayed from over here though, growing up, because it was the thing to do. This was more like the haunted area on the block, like you have abandoned houses in the movies and cartoons. Fake in reality but real in your head."

"So you lied? You didn't tell me the whole truth?"

"I just never saw it for myself, so I thought it was old wives tales. I'm not superstitious like that. I'm almost a grown man. What do I look like being scared of some stories? I just push through..." he explained, flexing his muscles before she cut him off.

"Get to the point, Mike."

"Look, go see the paper lady I told you about over there on the corner. You can't miss her."

"Mrs. Clance?"

"Yeah. She will tell you everything. She knows about it all, more than me. I'm not even supposed to talk about it, and from what I saw with you, I'm gonna keep it that way. You should, too. Tell your mom to move." He got back into the car, but she called him once more.

"Yeah?" he responded.

"Can I call you...please? I can tell you don't want to be around here, but can I just call you? I mean, you may be able to help me. I'm here all by myself most of the day."

"Yeah. Yeah, you can call me. No harm in that."

"I mean as soon as I go back inside."

"Sure, Dina. Yeah," he responded, giving in to her request. "Dina, I still like you, but this is just ..."

"Wait," she interjected. "Will you come with me?"

"Where?"

"To Mrs. Clance's." She looked back at her home. "I don't want to go back in there until I know more about this area."

"Look, I'll give you a lift over there, with my phone recording, so if you can't deal with that, then you can't get in. I need video evidence of me not doing anything to you because..."

"I get it," she said, cutting him off again. "Just give me a second to shut my window and get my key."

"Alright."

Dina could tell that he didn't want to do it, but she needed him to do it because she felt much safer. After racing to the back of the condo, she boosted herself onto the window sill, but before she went inside, there was shouting coming from somewhere, like people were fighting. Instead of going to investigate, she ignored it and went inside her bedroom. However, when she entered her bedroom, the shouting sounded like it was actually inside her home.

Dina grabbed her keys and made her way to the bedroom door to peek out into the broad hallway. No one was there, but the hollering match continued. It sounded like the people were inside her living room. Suddenly, something crashed, and Dina jumped back before grabbing a trusty stick her mom gave her to keep behind her door at all times for self-defense at their previous residence. She was thinking that some people must have climbed in through her bedroom window and were trashing her house.

Making sure her bedroom door was wide open so she could run and dash from the window if she had to, she moved toward the living room slowly, gripping the stick tightly, ready to swing. The screaming worsened and then when she looked around the wall and into the living room, just like no one was ever there, the screaming stopped. The place was empty.

Shaken, she dropped her stick as noisy whispers began to come from the front door. The whispers were words and phrases she didn't understand, so instead of remaining there, allowing her mind to play tricks on her, she dashed through her bedroom and exited the window. Dropping to the ground relieved, she leaned against the brick and covered her ears. Immediately, the whispers ceased. Before she heard anything else, she ran around the building as fast as she could run, jumping into the car with Michael.

"What's wrong?" Michael asked, aware that something was very off due to the rate in which she was breathing. "Do I need to take off?"

he asked, peering through his windshield for anyone chasing Dina.

"No, nothing's wrong. Just I was rushing because I didn't want you to wait so long after everything I did...the other day," she stammered. "To Mrs. Clance's?"

"Alright." He took a deep breath, and they headed over to her home. When they arrived, which was in less than a minute, Michael remained in the car.

"I've been here already you know. I mean I met her."

"I already figured that, which is why I'm sitting in the car."

"Michael, I..."

"You know what, Dina?" he interrupted, not interested in anymore requests, "I don't want to be involved in this. As much as I like you, there's a whole lot more I don't like about this *situation*, and I prefer to keep my mind on ball and making my way in this world than figuring out some stuff that has nothing to do with me. You know your way back right?"

Dina looked at his palms, and they were sweating. No longer the smooth talking guy she met, she knew something was terribly bad about what she was about to learn about where she lived, but she refused to push him anymore about it. She stepped from the car, thanked him for the ride, the proceeded to Mrs. Clance's front door.

"Dina, wait." It was Michael. He'd already left his car and began walking up to her as she prepared to knock on Mrs. Clance's door.

"Yeah?"

"I'm sorry about all this. To be honest," he hesitated, "I didn't think it was real until you... I really thought it was superstition that we all just started to believe in since we were children. I think I can find out more about..."

"Michael. What are you doing at my door?" The front door opened, and it was Mrs. Clance. "You haven't been around here in a while." She still hadn't looked at Dina while she spoke which made her feel slightly uncomfortable. "I see you brought the new girl."

Finally, she turned to face her. "Are you still alright over there?"

"Yes… I mean, I need to ask you some questions, Mrs. Clance. Are you busy right now, because if you are, I can come back?" she asked, still pondering over the question Mrs. Clance asked about if she was *still* alright as if she wasn't supposed to be.

"Come on inside. I don't have any food for you this morning."

"You ate over here?" Michael whispered, shocked that Dina's previous visit was so formal. He'd never even eaten at Mrs. Clance's.

"Sure she did," Mrs. Clance answered cheerfully before Dina got the chance. "She ate over here just the other morning, and apparently, she didn't have any major questions to ask me," she paused before taking a seat on her light pink recliner, "until now." Then, she stopped speaking, opting to only stare at Dina without moving an inch. There was an awkward tension in the air, like Mrs. Clance already knew why Dina was there, but felt the need to behave as if she didn't know at all.

"Mrs. Clance, I think you already know why I'm here."

"Don't think so much, sweetheart," she responded with a huge smile and a raspy tone. Just as quickly as the smile came, it left. "That's what's going on, isn't it? Your thoughts."

Dina glanced at Michael, feeling uneasy at what would potentially come to light in the conversation. "Sometimes, or since I moved there, I haven't been the same. It feels like I'm not alone in there. I mean, I live with my mom, but it feels like ..."

"There is someone else."

"Yes, ma'am."

"Who?"

"I don't know who, but they are there."

"They?"

"Yes ma'am. They make noise."

"From where?"

"Next door," she stammered, "From next door...across from us."

"Nobody lives there. Nobody has lived there for years, so what you're saying to me is a lie."

"I'm not lying, Mrs…"

"It's a lie!" She stood up and charged at Dina before suddenly halting, making direct eye to eye contact. "Now you tell me from where. Do you think I'm someone's fool, child?"

"Let me outta here," Dina replied, feeling very disrespected and refused to tolerate it. She pushed past Mrs. Clance, and before Michael got up to follow, Mrs. Clance responded loudly in an attempt to stop her.

"Seems like everybody I ever knew moved from there in two weeks time, young lady. They never could keep anyone over there. They either went crazy or they just left period. You and your mom are the only ones to be in there in years, maybe over ten years or so. Michael, you were in elementary school when the last people were there. It used to be a nice area over there where you live, same as the rest of us here in these condominiums."

"They tried to move people inside there many times, but they all left or vanished, leaving all of their stuff behind. Can you believe that? Word is that some went to a homeless shelter and preferred it. A homeless shelter over your own home?" she stressed, "But they never did say what happened. They just didn't want to talk about it. I remember asking about why and what, but never got the answers I needed." She looked at Michael and Dina as they stood there listening. "They just wanted peace. So us adults we kept piecing together stories trying to make sense of it all out of fear," she explained. "We were all scared, scared that what was rumored to be happening to them would happen to us soon because we live here, too, right nearby," she continued, nodding for them to take their seats again. They did. "We were so scared in fact that just like you did, Dina, we lied." Mrs. Clance then looked at Michael. "We told you that you would get kidnapped, and then we would say other things, worse things, but we never did tell the complete truth because we didn't know the complete truth. We just wanted everyone safe. I'm sure you got different stories, too, didn't you, Michael?"

"Yes ma'am," he responded to get it over with.

"Yes sir," she repeated. "I know you did because I did, too. That's why you're here. Because you assume I know more than everybody else." She leaned over from her recliner and continued, "Well, maybe I might, but maybe I don't at all. All I know is there was something or somebody over there before any of us even got here, at the start of this place being built. The first people to live here in this area...they lived right over there in your area, Dina. That was a long while ago, too. I wasn't even here yet," her voice traveled before she slightly digressed.

"Don't go thinking I'm fussing at you, Dina, but I've heard answers like that lie you gave me before. It throws me into a fit of frustration. Nobody lives across from you, right? When I tracked down the last people who tried to live there from way back, they said the same thing. Said somebody was over there, but nobody was there at the same time. There was even talk of some people vanishing. Now how can that be? I'm sorry for raising my voice. I'm just tired of the same ridiculous answers."

They all sat there quietly because everyone felt like they'd already said their piece. However, they all knew something was missing. That something needed to be said. Dina wanted to say it, but couldn't. She would sound crazy. People inside a peephole? To her relief, finally, Mrs. Clance broke the silence. "Wait right here."

Dina and Michael waited patiently in the living room while Mrs. Clance exited into the back rooms. Michael stood up as if he was about to sneak out, but Dina begged for him to stay, so he sat back down on the couch. Just as he did, Mrs. Clance returned with a sealed, white box. She cut it open with large, yellow-handled seamstress scissors. Removing the lid, Mrs. Clance revealed multiple sheets of paper and also newspaper clippings from the inside of the box, lining them across the coffee table so that Dina and Michael could see the clearly.

"These are the papers that I wrote about and documented myself along with other newspaper clippings pertaining to things that happened over there before I even moved here. The documents I wrote, no major papers wanted to publish, so I became my own publisher, and that's why I still do it today, but for the community." She then removed more papers from down inside the box. There were more of her notes. She had stacks of them.

"You and your mother may be the first people to move in there in over ten years, Dina, but there have been plenty times they've tried to keep people there before that. Each time they failed. I believe this is why they couldn't keep folks - fear. Fear of something. Fear of someone, someone before we got here." Mrs. Clance handed her the notes. "It's all legible and in order. I wrote the page numbers on the bottom just in case they ever got out of order."

"It's a lot. It's gonna take me... I mean, I thought you could probably just tell me the conclusion of your research and..."

"There's something over there, Dina," she ominously interrupted. "There's some secret. I can't prove it, but there is. Whatever it is that's making you feel that way, like you're seeing things, piece it together. You're the only one who can. You are the only person who can help me prove it."

"Why am I the only one?"

"Because you're the only one seeing it and going through it, just like the rest said they did." She sat back down in her recliner. "They just didn't tell the whole story because they would seem..."

"Crazy," Dina said under her breath. Michael heard her, but he chose to remain out of the conversation. As a matter of fact, he chose to end it.

"I have to...we have to go, Mrs. Clance. Thank you?" he asked as if he needed permission to leave. The situation was too much for him to grasp. Dina followed him out the door toting the box of papers, nodding good-bye to Mrs. Clance, and as Dina stepped out, he said, "And just to let you know, I'm not reading through that with you or anyone else. I'll drop you back at the house, and…"

"Wait what? What do you mean you aren't reading it with me? Come on, Mike," she argued. "Don't you want to know what's going on, including what happened and is actually happening to me?"

"Dina."

"Michael," she emphasized.

"Call me and let me know. I gotta go to the court."

"The court? You already know how to ball. Skipping a day won't hurt."

"Look what skipping a day got me so far," he said as he sat in the car and unlocked the door for Dina. When he noticed the door didn't open, he turned to see her walking away. Then, he jumped out. "Dina!"

"You said enough. I can walk. My feet are just as good as your wheels."

"Man, Dina, give me the box," he complained, catching up to her and taking it from her hands. "I didn't even mean it like that. Come on. Let me take you back, go play some ball, you know, get myself together. You're an athlete. You know how I have to have a clear head. Then, I'll stop back by. A couple of hours tops. Bring us some lunch. This superstitious stuff is getting too real to me. I'm starting to believe it," he whispered without Dina hearing it.

Dina stood there for a second and decided that it was a deal. "Okay. Just come to my back window. I'm not going to the front door. Call before you come so I can be on the lookout."

"Alright," he smiled. "Good. You know how to make a brother feel guilty." He walked back over with her to the car, opened the door for her and then got into the car, dropping her off back home.

CHAPTER 6

As she entered her bedroom and shut the window, she became relieved that everything was as she left it. There was absolutely no noise anywhere in the condo. She was thirsty, so she took a deep breath and made her way to the kitchen, feeling a bit more confident that others had been through the same situation that she'd been through. It felt better knowing that it wasn't her imagination or that she probably wasn't mentally ill.

As she made her way back to her bedroom with the glass of water, some of it spilled on the floor. The sound rippled like it dropped into a large body of water, causing Dina to stop in her tracks. She knew the sound was odd and completely impossible, therefore, she didn't want to entertain it. Without looking down, she continued walking rapidly until she reached her room again. She shut and locked the door, then she looked down.

"Thank God," she sighed, relieved that she wasn't visualizing an ocean beneath her feet. She'd seen so many things that didn't make sense until she didn't want to inspect anything else.

Finally sitting on her bed and feeling safe inside the room, she sat her glass of water down beside the bed and began sifting through the handwritten pages of documents. It looked like hundreds, some that were halfway done but some that were two and three pages long. There were dates at the top, but then she saw newspaper clippings and full articles that wrote about one specific family. That was where she started, until she heard the door slam. The noise startled her until she heard her mother's voice. A huge smile came across her face as she put everything back in the box and placed it near her closet.

"Mom!"

She burst through her room door like she was small child. Seeing her mother was a breath of fresh air. "That's what you wore to work today?"

"Yeah, I took a change of clothes with me. I figured I would come home early and see about you. I let the boss know you weren't feeling too well. How are you?"

"I'm better. Uhmm, I invited Michael back over," she stated, wanting to clear the air before he came. She realized that her mother didn't care for him much after what happened, and she was still probably suspicious of him still. "He'll be coming in a couple of hours, and maybe you can meet him?"

"Sure, baby. Listen, I want us to do something."

Dina stood there shocked at her mom's response to Michael's coming over, but she didn't argue with it. Instead, she walked over so she could get an earful of what her mom had planned.

"I was thinking about it, and I think we should confront whatever it is bothering you.

Why should I believe a psychiatrist over you, my own daughter? So let's go."

"What?" Dina asked confused.

"We're going over there," she said with a smile.

"Over where?"

"Over there. I have the combination."

"I know somebody that knows somebody. The combinations to those locks are generic."

Dina giggled in disbelief that her mother was actually going to open the condo next door. "Are you serious? You're actually going over there? Mom, you're kidding, right?"

"No. If someone is over there playing games, flicking on lights and other things, they will be cited or arrested. Simple solution, right? I have permission to view a property. They don't. Besides, the realtor is meeting us. She's on the way. We can go on in. You ready?"

"Of course, I'm ready!" Dina stated excitedly. "Mom, thank you! Thank you so much. Let me put my shoes back on. I'm coming. At least we can rule this out face to face!" Dina was ecstatic. By the time she went back into the living room, her mother was already at the front door of the other condo, putting in the combination. She walked up behind her. "Ma, shouldn't we ring the bell first just in case?"

Her mother turned the knob after removing the lock. "Nope." The door swung open. "We're inside now." As she walked in, she didn't turn to wait on Dina to follow. She just strolled in and told her to close the door behind her. Dina did as instructed and then called out, "Hello?"

The house had a moist smell, like there was a leak somewhere either in the floor or the roof. As Dina walked around, the home was the same layout as her own except the other way around. She then began to envision all the violence she'd seen in the peephole exactly where she was standing.

Dina stared at the floor and watched it all again in her mind's eye. Shivers crawled down her spine like ants on the crack of a sidewalk. She shook as she felt an eerie presence behind her, but when she turned around, no one was there, neither was her mother.

"Mom?" she called, believing that she'd only stepped back into the bedrooms. Therefore, she made her way back there, peeping into each room, but she didn't see her mother anywhere. "Mom?" she called as she moved back toward the front living area, but as she walked, she noticed shadows moving her way through her periphery. She locked eyes with their presence, and they halted suddenly before erupting into high-pitched wails. Dina ran for the only escape there was – the front door - as their screeching elevated in volume. The wailing shadows remained in place as Dina struggled to open the door, but it was sealed shut.

"Mom! Mom!" Sweat poured from her forehead as she shouted feverously for her mother,forcefully yanking on the doorknob, but it refused to turn. "Help me!" she screamed as the breath from the shadows' wails blew between the curls of her thick hair.

"What's wrong, baby?" The wailing stopped. It was her mother responding from behind, but when Dina turned around, something was very wrong. "Mom?" As she spoke, her mother's facial skin began to sliding off on one side. Dina jumped to aid her mother, trying to push her mother's skin back into the proper area on her face, but everything she tried was ineffective. The skin was just dropping, oozing through her fingers.

Her mother cried in agony as her skin dripped like frozen ice cream on a summer day. Dina's sanity crumbled as the skin failed to adhere and made its way down the back of her hands like hot slime. Her mother continued to disfigure as even more loose skin from the other side of her face dropped to the floor and into her hands before revealing the bare, bloody muscles and skeleton. During all of the pain, her mother's agony unexplainably turned to laughter before the giggles were stifled when she began to choke on something unknown caught inside her throat. There were bugs. They began crawling from her mouth, plugging anymore sound from escaping. In a fit of hysteria, Dina fell backwards, but through the door, as if it wasn't ever there at all. Her body banged against the cement walkway as she hollered uncontrollably, shoving her way backwards until her back slammed against the front door of her condo. She scrambled getting up as her decrepit faced mother stood there at the doorway trying to talk before someone called Dina's name. The door then slammed shut. It was Michael who ran to her side, hearing her screaming like she was being attacked.

"Dina! What the hell? Dina? Dina, Dina, wait, wait," he stammered as he avoided her swipes and punches at his face while he searched around to see who attacked her. "Dina! It's me. Stop hitting, come on now. Dina, stop!" He finally shouted, about to leave her there, becoming overly concerned about his own welfare.

Finally, she focused on him, slowly returning to reality as she rubbed her hands roughly against the concrete. Mike looked on in horror, finally restraining her before she ripped her skin.

"Dina, you're gonna hurt yourself," he explained as he lightly grabbed both her wrists.

"I need to go in the house. I need to go back in!" she screamed repeatedly, snatching her wrists from his hands, realizing finally that they weren't covered in her mother's melted skin.

"Just open it!" Michael shouted, confused and also frustrated, so he reached around her and turned the knob. The door opened, and she ran inside, tumbling to the floor, flipping her hands over constantly double and triple checking them to be certain they were clean. She then began holding her head, rocking back and forth, moaning and mentally tortured by everything that had occurred.

Michael stood at the doorway watching fear morph her into a whole other being for minutes, curling into a ball, twitching and wiping tears away so she could see clearly that she was safe. He didn't move from the doorway. He only watched until Dina finally spoke.

"Don't leave me in here. Please, don't leave me in here alone," she cried, balled up on the floor. "My mom was here...my mom."

"Your mom?"

"Where is my mom?"

"I don't know. She's not around here."

"She's...she was right across from me. Her face and she..."

"May I come in, Dina?"

"Yes, and please close the door. Please," she begged. "Just close the door," she wept. "It wasn't my mom. I thought it was my mom. She was in here, and I followed her. There's a realtor coming..." she rambled, but Michael didn't know what she was talking about.

"Do I need to call your mom for you?" He looked around. "Where's your phone?"

"It's in my room," she said, sitting up on the floor with her back against the sofa. "You don't have your cell phone?" she asked curiously.

"It's in my car." Michael answered, before initiating his search for her home phone. "Which room?"

148

"It's the one on the left."

He went down the hall, searched her room and returned with the telephone. "What's the number?"

"Don't call her."

"What? Why not? You're upset."

"But you don't understand. I just need you to stay with me, okay? Please, just until my mom...I need to look outside to make sure my mom's car isn't out here." She got up from the floor and looked out of the window. Her mother's car wasn't in the designated parking space meaning that it wasn't her mom with her at all. It was someone else, something else and it had led her into the other condo.

Quickly, she ran back to Michael, begging and pleading with him not to leave her alone. He stood there, stoic for seconds, before trying to calm her with his touch. She started to cry but found comfort as she rested against his chest. As he saw that she was being soothed, he rubbed her back and took her to the sofa to sit down.

"Tell me what happened, Dina."

She desperately looked into his eyes. "Mom came inside, and we were supposed to be meeting a realtor over there according to what she told me. Mom, she had the combination and everything to get inside the condo, but when we got in somehow, Mom disappeared. When I went to look for her, I wasn't alone in there. Dark shadows or ghosts started crying, and the closer I got to the door, the louder the crying got. Then, I finally heard my mom behind me but when I turned around, it was her, but then her skin..."

"What?"

"Her skin slid from her face and there was some desecrated body behind it. She was laughing but then bugs and more bugs came from her throat."

He got up from the sofa and walked toward the front door to look out the peephole. "Dina, the lock is on the door over there."

"Michael, I was in there! I was in there!"

"How long were you in there?"

"Like five minutes. When you left, it wasn't even ten minutes before my mom came home, and that's when we went inside."

He walked back over to her. "Dina, that can't be right."

"Why not? I'm not crazy. I know what hap..."

"I've been gone for at least an hour and a half."

"What?" she asked, backing away from him.

"Yeah. I've been gone. Stopped at the store and decided to come over earlier than planned. I heard you screaming in the corridor when I pulled up, and that was when I jumped out of my car because it sounded like someone was attacking you."

Dina walked over to the house phone and looked at the time, and Michael began to speak again. "See what time it is."

He was right. He'd been gone for nearly two hours. Dina's mind floated into chaos. She was lost. Her reality wasn't reality, and her concept of time was scattered, but she wasn't dreaming. Michael was in front of her, just like her mother was and the weeping shadows in the other condo. Tears drifted down her face, and again, Michael stood there and watched until suddenly, she took a deep breath, shook her body, and grabbed hold to all the precious courage she had left and urged him.

"Michael, come with me to my room. We have to look through those papers." She grabbed his wrist, and he allowed her to guide him back into her bedroom. "Here," she started, pulling out the box of notes. "I found something beneath the pages of notes. They were real articles of some people, and I bet it's the people who used to live here."

"Pull it out," Michael stated while peeping over his shoulder suspiciously. Dina saw him.

"It's fine. It's fine. Here, I have a small recorder I use in class." She walked over, slightly irritated, believing that he looked over his shoulder out of paranoia that he would be accused, pulled out her own voice activated recorder and hit record, "See," she explained, shaking it in front of his face, "That way, I can't set you up. I can't set him up!" she yelled, her voice going directly into the recorder.

"Chill, Dina," he smiled. "It's not what you think." Then, his smile faded, and his eyes became distant and cold. "Really. It isn't paranoia at all." However, she paid him no attention and continued talking into the recorder.

"I'm just in here seeing things that aren't real from next door or wherever...like in a peephole!" she continued, "And we're both about to sit on my bed, not have sex, but read! Michael hasn't laid a finger on me in any way," she sang, "So leave him alone. Instead, try and find the freaks inside my door!" She peeked back up at him as she laid out all the newspapers across the bed and smirked, pushing back against the fear moments earlier since Michael was there with her. She needed him to be comfortable around her because she felt much safer with him there, and she was willing to do just about anything.

As soon as he saw that Dina was trying to fight her fears, he reached for her hand to assure her.

"It's gonna be okay, Dina. I'm sorry about not being..."

"I understand. It's not your fault. It's not mine either. I know I'm not completely crazy. Nobody who lived here was, and I'm gonna figure it out."

"We're gonna figure it out, Dina. I won't leave you anymore, alright?"

She smiled as he took her other hand and kissed her on her cheek. She then kissed him back on his lips. "We can keep this part on the recorder. I kissed you voluntarily."

He took a deep breath and laughed, "Let's get started then."

They both sat on the bed and started reading through all the material. There was one longer article in particular that really caught Dina's attention due to the caption beneath the photo which read *"Missing couple and children, still not found."*

In faded black and white, there were the children and their mom, along with their father who stood behind them all in a holiday portrait. Dina ran her hand across the picture. It was them. It was really them.

"Michael."

"Yeah? What's up?"

"That's them."

"Who?"

"Them."

Suddenly, there was a huge noise at the front door. When she became startled but Michael didn't, she knew it was for her. She ignored it for a while, pretending to read the paper but really listening to the raging noise from the living room. As Michael read, she got up.

"I'll be back. I have to go to the bathroom. I'll be right back."

"Alright. I'm right here. Not going anywhere. I'm never going anywhere."

Dina smiled at his loyal gesture and left the room, leaving Michael behind to scan through the newspapers, but he didn't. Instead, he sat up on the bed, cocked his head downward toward the floor, listening to her every step. An unhinged smile crept across his face, and he slowly slide the newspapers to the side of the bed and rocked back and forth as if he was in waiting...for something unknown.

Dina cleared the room and made her way toward the front door once again determined to fight back against what had already began to torment her, especially now that Michael was in the back room and on her side. She felt more secure. Most of all, she was determined to find out more. Therefore, she peered through the peephole, and the bangs on the door stopped, pulling her into another scene.

"Mommy!" shouted the same little girl she'd seen before but this time the tension in the room was reminiscent of death. "Mommy!"

Gripping the knob and bracing herself against the door, Dina continued watching as the little girl's mother lay there in the middle of the floor unconscious. Her daughter was trying to pull her arm in order to move her but couldn't because her mother was too heavy. Then, there were more noises, like something being thrown against the wall. It kept pounding and pounding until the little girl wound up watching her brother being thrown to the floor beside their mother lifeless.

She cried, stumbling over her brother while attempting to wake him up by shaking him wildly by his arms and waist. Dina buckled at the sight of it all and angrily shouted, "Leave her alone!" The man walked inside the room, and stood over little girl's body as she pleaded with her only brother to come back to life.

"No! Leave her alone!" At Dina's screams, the man raised his head, stared into the peephole and grinned. He saw her.

"Dina!" Michael shouted, running around the corner as she stood there at the door screaming. He forcefully pulled her from the door and looked through the peephole himself.

"He's gonna kill her!" she screamed. "He just killed that little boy, Michael! And he saw me! He looked right at me."

"Dina, who? Who?" he asked as he continued searching inside the peephole. "Who?" he finally yelled, growing agitated, his anger swelling to a point where Dina didn't even recognize him. His behavior had done a complete change. He'd become vicious instead of compassionate, out of control instead of in control, as he kept demanding believable answer from Dina that she couldn't answer as such. Therefore, she slightly backed away, pondering fearfully if he was fuming at her or at the situation. Then, she finally answered his question.

"The man in the peephole. He just killed him, and he's gonna kill her," she whimpered. "Mike, he saw me. He looked right at me."

"Dina," Michael spoke, as he continued to peep out of the peephole as she looked on. Michael's head began moving from right to left oddly like a pendulum, as he checked the peephole with both eyes. It appeared like he was playing some type of game. Then, he called her again, singing it in a tune. "Dina." Each time his head moved to one side, he called her name, calling her name to the beat of the motion of his head. As his head swung right, he sang the first half of her name, and when it went left, he sang the second syllable.

"Michael?" She stepped closer, reaching forward to touch his shoulder. "Michael, what's wrong?"

His head stopped moving. "I think I have a crook in my neck, Dina," he explained, grinning from ear to ear. When her hand touched his shoulder, there was a loud pop and then many cracks as his neck broke. Every bone shattered as his neck twisted backwards until Michael laid eyes on the person he wanted to see. "Dina," the mangled Michael called in a totally different voice, "Can you help me like you're asking me to help you? Look at me, Dina," he stated as Dina screamed in horror. He stepped toward her, but she'd become frozen in fear as his body staggered, his arms reaching forward but in the opposite direction like he was trying to grab her but confused on how his arms were reaching the wrong way. He began to run into the walls, out of control as his body contorted in a multitude of disfiguring ways. Completely out of control, the unfamiliar voice transformed back to Michael's voice, and the sound of tumultuous pain overtook the evil one that gripped it seconds ago.

"Dina!" Michael yelled as his body banged against the walls. "What's wrong with me?"

"Michael!" Dina screamed before she watched him fall lifelessly to the floor, shaking and foaming at the mouth. "Michael!" She immediately fell to the floor, unable to touch him because his body had been destroyed from the inside out. She hovered over him as he struggled immensely to stay alive, and as her hand lightly grazed his skin, he moaned terribly, his eyes rolling to the back of his head as his arms became limp, crashing to the floor as his own neck strangled him, having twisted a full one hundred and eighty degrees. Finally, Michael stopped moving completely. He was dead.

"Oh God! Oh God, please, no. Michael! Wake up, please!" she begged he lay dead there before her. Would the same thing happen to her? Would she be the next to die?

The walls began to close in on her, and her mouth grew pasty as nausea engulfed her entire digestive tract, but as she fell away, Michael's eyes opened, and he grabbed her ankle, forcibly dragging her back with the full strength of ease.

Dina fought back, kicking with her other leg while calling for someone, anyone to rescue her. Michael banged her leg against the floor like it was a paper weight as she struggled to keep any distance between them. As she fought, she noticed that it wasn't Michael any longer. Michael's face had already somehow disappeared, but another face was there. It was the man from the peephole, and he had evil laced across his eyes as he glared back at her. He was trying to kill her. She'd been deceived again, or was it that the deception had never stopped?

"Help me!" The walls mocked her cries, echoing in the background. No matter how loudly she screamed, no one heard her. She only heard herself, like she was inside a bubble. There was no one. She was going to die.

"Get off me! Get off me," Dina fought, growing angrier with the knowledge that she was on her own. The only way she would get out was through a vicious fight, so she gave him one. Instead of pulling away from him, she sprang toward the man who continued to berate her with laughter until he transformed again before her eyes, turning back into Michael.

With murder in his eyes, he grabbed her by her throat, shoving the back of her head into the floor until he suddenly disappeared into thin air, leaving the front door to open, exposing her to her mother, her real mother, coming through the door to see her only daughter struggling on the floor with her own hands wrapped around her neck.

THE PEEPHOLE

CHAPTER 7

"Mama?" Dina backed away frightened with each step her mother took toward her as if her mother was a complete stranger. Grace perceived the fear in Dina's eyes, and she went down to the floor to crawl to her but stopped mid-crawl as Dina continued to move away from her more rapidly than before.

"Dina, baby. It's me. It's Mama, baby. Please," she pleaded, needing to comfort her distraught daughter, "Come over here so I can check on you. I'm not coming any closer to you. I'll let you come to me. Dina, baby, your neck…" her mother stated as helplessness overtook her.

"Get away from me! You get away from me. Who are you? You aren't my mom," she shouted, having flashbacks of her mother's skin pealing from her face. "You were already here earlier, and Michael, he was already here. You locked me in there. You told me…" she stammered, slamming her hands into the floor. "You told me!"

"Dina, listen to me," she responded carefully and calmly. "I haven't been home earlier. I don't know what you're talking about, baby, but I'm at home now, and I just got here. I haven't been home all day long. Did that boy come here again?" she asked, growing even more furious because she was starting to connect the dots between him and her daughter's erratic behavior.

"Mama?" she cried, hoping it was really her. "He was here, but then he was right there." She pointed to the area on the floor next to her mother. "He was just right there on the floor, just now, and his arms were backwards and his head... then he changed into another man. He was the man in the peephole. He attacked me. Mama, he was trying to kill me, and then he disappeared," she exclaimed, "He was just right here before you came inside, and he just disappeared! It wasn't really Michael, but then it was. I don't know!"

"You're not making any sense, baby."

"I know what I'm telling you!" she screamed, grabbing her head, beating it with her hands as hard as she could near her temples, when her mother rushed over to stop her.

"Stop it! Just stop it before you kill yourself! Dina, this is me. I'm your mother. Stop!" She struggled to hold her down until Dina grew exhausted of screaming and fighting. That was when there was a knock on the door. Whoever it was kept knocking, and then there was a voice on the other side.

"Mama! Mama! Don't go over there. Just stay over here with me. Let's just go to the back."

"I'm going to see who it is..."

"Wait, Mom, you hear it?"

"Don't you?"

Dina knew the knock was real then. It had to be, and as her mother went to answer the front door, Dina tensed up, holding on to the corner of the wall, trembling, awaiting what would happen next.

""May I help you?" she asked the young man standing at the door.

"How are you doing, ma'am? My name is Michael DeMonte. Is Dina available? I came by to help her look through some papers we..."

"I remember your face now. I saw you from far away. Were you over here today?"

"No ma'am. You mean inside? No," he stated as he glanced at an out of sorts Dina clinging to the floor. "Is everything alright?"

"You tell me."

Michael shrugged and backed away a couple of paces realizing quickly that he was subtly being accused. "I got nothing to tell. I just came over here like I promised Dina I would and ..."

"Ma, I don't think he was really here. I thought you were here, too. Neither of you were." She then turned to look at the clock. The time had gone by...hours...but it felt like minutes. "Mama, I asked him to come," she whispered in an attempt to sort out her own thoughts.

Her mother grew quiet before inviting him to speak, changing her tone. "Can you tell me what happened to my daughter today and the other day? You can come on in. I'm not accusing you of anything, Michael," she explained apologetically, realizing that her tone was harsh, but she remained suspicious at the same time. Since Dina reiterated the fact that he hadn't done anything wrong, she felt it was the wise thing to do to let him inside so she could find out more information. Maybe he could verify all Dina was trying to explain to the doctor and make some sense of it. "I just came in and found her distraught, and I don't know what's going on. Please...and I'm so sorry for how I came off, but can you tell me anything. I'm just concerned about her. It's like she is spiraling out of control." She fully opened the door and invited him inside. He shook his head, dropped it low, but hesitantly entered.

"Look, about the other day ... all I know is she went toward the front door, screaming, shouting something, and the next thing I knew was that she was literally on the door. I'm not figuratively saying what I'm saying. She was plastered, just like this," he demonstrated, "On the door. By the time I jumped out the window, her feet were elevated from the floor, like she was hanging up there by a door hook. I'm not gonna stand here and lie." He looked down at Dina on the floor with her head low, feeling ashamed. "I was afraid. I mean, I have a lot to lose if people thought I'd done something to her." Then, he crouched down next to her. "But I'm not afraid anymore. What's happening has nothing to do with Dina," he continued, glancing back up at her mother. "This isn't the first time stuff like this has happened. It might not be the last either. There's something in this place, only this place, and if you don't get out of here really soon, you may never leave the same or at all."

"What do you mean?" Grace asked, nodding him in the direction of the sofa as he helped Dina up from the floor. Grace moved to hold her daughter, and they both sat together on the sofa to listen to what Michael had to say, Dina cradled in her arms.

"My mom, she didn't want to say anything about it. Instead of going to play ball and clear my head, I went to talk to my mom. She told me the full truth this time, but only because I told her that you're my friend, Dina," he expressed empathetically. "She cried as soon as I told her that you were my friend and what happened to you at the door. She knew I cared for you and didn't want anything to happen to you." He wiped his face with the palm of his hand, sighed and continued, pushing through the tension. "I'm not even supposed to be here. She wanted me to tell Dina this whole story away from here," he continued to explain, moving his eyes around the condo. "She took me out back and told me the real story, one that she'd never told me before, and right before telling me, she forced me to promise never to ask her about it again." He paused. "It's not a superstition, Dina...Mrs. Grace. It's real."

"My mom, she was the caretaker of this elderly lady named Miss Jasmine, who never liked to be called by her last name. That lady named Jasmine was a cousin of the person who used to live here, even before I was born. When Jasmine found out where my mom lived, she started telling my mom stories, but there was one story that made Jasmine cry. After she told my mom, my mom found out that she was the first person she ever told the full truth about it. She made mom swear never to tell, and she never did. She pretended and made things up, but never told all she knew. Mom said we would have moved away from here, but couldn't afford it. She still can't."

"Anyway, my mom found out about how the lady who apparently used to live next door to where you two live now would become terrified sometimes. She would call old, Miss Jasmine in the middle of the night crying, but she never would say what was wrong. She would say she just needed someone to listen to her cry. Old Miss Jasmine would do it, too. Listen to her cry."

"Now, if I'm repeating this right," Michael continued, clearing his throat, "The dude she was living with went crazy on her. That dude was Miss Jasmine's blood cousin. The lady was cousin by marriage. Anyway, he beat his wife so bad that she tossed her children from the back window once when he was in a frenzy just to keep them safe. She followed them out the window in the middle of the night. By the time he realized they were gone from the condo, they were already out of sight. After that, Ma said that old Miss Jasmine told her that the woman and children returned. The man was fine for a while. Before long though, they had financial problems to add to the abuse, and he couldn't pay for the roof over his head. He was getting kicked out. That was when the lady started calling old Miss Jasmine again, crying at night. Then one day, she stopped calling and crying for good. He killed them and himself."

"What has that got to do with us and our condo? We don't live there?" Grace stressed, referring to the condo next door.

"There was a note left before he took his life. Old lady Jasmine was the next of kin. They were the last two alive of their small family. Word was that death followed their family, taking them out in groups or one by one like a curse came specifically to destroy them all. Before he killed himself, he called Miss Jasmine. He told her he was about to shoot himself and that he loved her but no one was gonna put him out anymore. Said he was tired and he wasn't gonna let a curse choose for him. He was gonna choose. That was when old lady Jasmine got a ride over here, I suppose believing that she could keep him from doing what he promised he was going to do – kill everybody in his family. I don't know what happened next, but before the cops got there, old lady Jasmine had already gone inside, found the note and seen all their dead bodies. She kept that note. It was addressed to her, so she felt it wasn't their business. Never gave it to the cops. Since she knew that my mom would be her last caretaker, she showed it to her."

"What was on the note?"

"My mom refused to tell me the exact words, but it had haunted my mom ever since. All mom told me today was that the man who killed his family and himself was never leaving. She knew it was real because old lady Jasmine told her to pray and pray hard whenever there was a murder suicide, something about a spell being left on the place, all because he refused to leave. Something about when a spirit departs unwillingly or in turmoil from the body, it will never be torn apart from the place where the body fell dead. Old lady Jasmine told my mom that spirits were doing that since she was a child, and that was what was always going to happen here – there would be angry, lost souls somewhere here, that would find a place to hide, in the walls, floor…wherever. That main soul, the one who caused the death, would be here forever, as the troubled guardian. He won't let any of the others leave, and he will take who he desires forever. Nobody can do anything about it.

This place where you live isn't the territory of the living. It's the territory of the dead."

Michael stood up. "I'm not sure why it's affecting this condo, too, Mrs. Grace, but it is."

Grace stood up to face Michael. "What are you saying?"

"I'm saying that this really is true. Dina, we need to look through those articles..."

"No, no...not today. I'll call you," she stammered. "I'll call you."

"What articles?" Grace inquired, glancing at the both of them, awaiting an answer. "Well?"

"We went to Mrs. Clance's."

"Who's that?"

"She had some articles that she gave us to try and figure out this whole thing."

"Is she some witch?"

"No, no ma'am. She's not a witch or anything like that. She just researched it for a long time and felt like Dina could help her put the pieces together for why this is happening and has happened to..."

"Well, my child isn't helping anyone with anything! Do you hear me? You can go tell Mrs. Clance what you told us, and she'll know about all of this through you and your mother," Grace snapped, feeling deeply offended that someone whom she didn't know had her child researching some curse and believing that the whole problem stemmed from that research. "You can leave now, Michael. Don't come back here. And for the record, I'm not superstitious nor will I listen to some old tale told by some dead woman named Jasmine who found a note next door from her crazy cousin!" It was all too much for Grace. The information was not only new but literally unbelievable, so she didn't want to discuss it nor believe it. She refused.

"Please..."

"Leave," Grace ordered firmly as Dina began screaming against her mother's wishes. As far as Michael, he left quietly.

Her mother slammed the door shut behind Michael, and Dina rose from the couch teary-eyed and full of rage at her mother. "Mom, he was trying to help. He is telling you the truth. It makes sense."

"It makes no sense! I taught you better than to get involved with people who dip and dap in witchcraft."

"Mom, Michael isn't involved in anything like that! He didn't even want to help me to begin with! He actually changed his mind, putting himself at risk *for me*! He barely even knows me, and this is how you treat him?"

"I don't know what to believe coming from you or him, Dina, but I know one thing, good or bad, he won't be helping you any longer." She moved around the couch and picked up her purse from the floor. "Got you doing things and believing in..."

"Mom! I know what I saw! Before I even went anywhere with him. *You* don't even know what I saw!"

"That's because I know it's all fake. That's all you *and* I need to know."

"Mom, you'd already come home! You took me in there!" she exclaimed pointing in the direction of the condo next door. "You! But then you changed into some monster!"

"Shut up, Dina. Just hush! You heard all this weird stuff and now it's coming to life in your head. You're making it real," Grace stated as she held on to the wall feeling out of breath from all the fussing. "Let's just eat and go to sleep. I'm already ticked off enough from you going to see strange people that you told me nothing about, and then you don't even know their influence. They could have drugged you. You were attacking yourself, Dina! You were on the floor when I came in, and you had both your hands around your own throat! I saw you. No one was in here with you. No one! You didn't even recognize me!"

"I wasn't drugged! Listen to me!"

Shocked at Dina's tone and how she stood with her fists balled, shaking and barely able to control herself, Grace knew what she had to do. She had to calm the situation, so she walked forward to touch Dina affectionately on her shoulder, however, Dina saw right through it.

She knew her mother didn't believe her. It was a psychologist tactic where they behave as if they hear a patient when they really don't. It's just about maintaining control of the patient and calming the situation. Therefore, she moved her shoulder before her mother touched it and stormed down the hallway, slamming her bedroom door in clear defiance of her mother.

CHAPTER 8

Pages of Mrs. Clance's notes were scattered across the room, and she read. She read through all of her frustration. She read until she fell asleep that night. She didn't eat, and when she awakened, she realized she'd fallen asleep on the hard floor with the most important paper in her hand. It was the article that wrote about the scene of the murder-suicide.

The article described three people piled onto each other, a mother and her children, but there was another body, a man's remains, lying dead beside the others with a gunshot wound to his head. Dina realized that she'd already seen what happened up to a point, with her own eyes through the peephole, but she didn't see the rest – none of what Michael said happened with old lady Jasmine entering the scene and neither did she see the man kill himself.

There was a picture of all the victims. The woman had short curly hair, styled wonderfully with the sides shaven which fit her face excellently. The little girl, who sat confidently on her lap like she was born to take photos, showed off her pigtails bedazzled with barrettes. There was also the son who stood right next to his mother like a big boy, proud of his suit and tie that matched his father's who stood behind them all, his arms seeming more a protective space for them instead of a harmful place.

The man was handsome, with a palpable confidence which radiated through the photo. His smile wasn't there but it showed in another way – through his eyes. One could tell he was proud of where he was in life unlike when she saw him in the peephole before he murdered his family and took his own life. The man she saw then was a lonely man, trapped in his own world, belittled by life and angry to the point of evil at everything and everyone in sight. He was losing everything, including control, and he decided he wasn't going to let that happen.

Dina dropped the paper to the floor, and it blew all the way to the opposite wall like a draft lifted and carried it away. Plastered against the wall, the portrait stared back at her and she at it as her lamp flickered for a couple seconds, prompting Dina to stand and twist the bulb a bit tighter. The light shone brightly again, and Dina gave herself a nice stretch, reaching as far as she could toward the ceiling before dropping her arms to her side.

She thought about the argument she had with her mother, and the guilt weighed her heart down like a boulder. Her mother wasn't aware of all she'd seen, and she finally realized that her mother probably didn't know what to think after walking into the home and finding her on the floor struggling for her life. After thinking about it, she realized that she didn't place herself in her mom's shoes, which wasn't fair. Above all else, she loved her mother, and she'd never gone to bed angry like that before because no day was promised to anyone. Therefore, she took a deep breath and opened her bedroom door to crawl in bed with her mother, however, when she opened the door, there was no hallway. Instead, she'd opened the door to a duplicate of her bedroom.

"What?" She spun around confused to see that the bedroom behind her was gone, bricked up into a full wall. She placed her hands on it, trying to find a way to get back, but there was no way, no matter how hard she shoved against it.

She then turned back around and saw her bedroom door on the other side of the duplicate bedroom. She ran to open the door. As she did, the same thing happened, except this time, when she turned to run back, there wasn't a wall blocking her, it was a door with a peephole. It was her own front door. It was broken around the edges and rusted, old and dirty. There was a shadow from within, beckoning her to look inside.

Startled and confused, Dina backed away, falling inside the new bedroom. She then rushed again to the bedroom door, flinging it open, and this time, she didn't look back. She only continued running forward, each time opening the bedroom door in front of her, until she finally opened up the final door. She then faced the peephole, but it had enlarged. It was so big that she could step directly through it with ease. The peephole had become an entrance, and through the entrance, at the end of the hallway stood a man, the man she knew as the one who shot everyone including himself - the man that old Miss Jasmine was related to, and the one that everyone in the community feared, except didn't know it.

She backed away but hit a brick wall which began to push her forward. "Mom! Mom, help me!" she screamed as the wall mercilessly shoved her forward as she scraped her palms and fingernails against the brick until they bled, tolerating the pain just to keep from tumbling into the place she didn't want to go, just to keep from going towards him.

All her fighting was of no use. She fell into the peephole as the man made his way slowly towards her. There was nowhere for her to run as she faced the man who'd continued to come after her since she moved in, posing as her mother and then posing as Michael. However, this time, there was no emulation. It was him.

"Leave me alone," she cried stumbling as she shoved the walls that surrounded her, searching for a way out. She pleaded for him to let her leave, promising to go and never return, but suddenly, he vanished.

Flustered, Dina madly scanned the room, desperate for a way out, but when she stepped away from the large peephole, it had already shrunk. It was her front door again, and the small peephole was there all over again. She quickly ran to peer back through it. On the other side was her mother, asleep in the bed.

"Mama!" she shouted, kicking the door but it was cemented into the wall. There was no way to open it. The doorknob was missing. "Mom! Please, wake up! Please," she screamed as she backed away from the peephole until finally, at her loudest and most vulnerable state, she shouted, "Get me out of here!"

Suddenly, like a spider on its web, a new presence crept up behind her. The sensation of another person lurked like a magnet to her skin, but she failed to turn around, paralyzed by the fear of knowing that it could have been him. In fact, she knew it was him. She stopped breathing, and over the sound of her pulsating heart, he spoke.

"Your mother can't get you out because I won't let you leave," he stated in a low voice that traveled with a huge gust of wind into her ears. His hands wrapped around her arms, and he shoved her through the door, directly into her mother's bedroom.

"Mom," she cried as she rushed over and dropped to her knees at the side of the bed. Her mother was sound asleep and hadn't heard any commotion. "Mom, wake up." Placing her head down on the sheets, Dina wiped her tears as she shook her mom's arm. "Mom?" Her mother wasn't moving, and her face was turned in the opposite direction. From there, Dina inspected the sheets for breathing motion. She wasn't breathing.

Dina sprang into action, leaping across the bed to the other side of her mother's motionless body, but as she threw back the covers, her mom's skeleton lie there as maggots dropped from her bones onto the mattress. The maggots fell atop Dina's face, hair and body, and she tumbled backwards off of the bed, banging her head against the wall, as the maggots seemed to multiply the more she shook them off. They just kept coming and coming until she finally broke down, running back to her own bedroom door furiously, kicking it open as the maggots dropped to the floor.

"Get off of me!" She slapped her face, hair and body until she was certain the maggots were gone, but when she became more aware of her surroundings, she had nowhere to go. She saw that her window was boarded up. She was trapped inside. Terror pushed her onto the bed and into the corner, shaking and silenced by fear in her own home, or was it?

As she sat there, the sound of paper rustled above her head. Terrified, she rolled her eyes upward to find all the newspapers that were once inside that white box stuck to the ceiling, but they weren't in random order. Each one told the story of the man and his family, but then when she reached the last newspaper clipping, it showed her face along with her mother's beneath the headline – Missing Teen and Mother Presumed Dead.

Her closet door then slowly opened, and her lamp flickered before going completely out. The bedroom was pitch black, and Dina was both terrified, confused and heartbroken over her mother. Her mother was already dead, according to the papers on the ceiling. Was her mother really dead? Was she now all alone, and she was next?

She squeezed her knees to her chest and watched the closet door continue to creep open as her eyes adjusted to the chaotic darkness. The creeks from the closet door created havoc in her mind as she blocked the sound from her ears. A painful psychosis gripped her as she began to hallucinate, shuddering at things not there and jumping from one side of the bed to another whenever there was the sound of what she thought could have been movement. In an instant, her body became extremely tense from the faint sound of breathing to her right side and then at her left.

Shifting in horror, she searched the darkness, but only darkness spoke back. The breathing persisted until she finally tore away from her post to only be restrained by two hands tugging her wrists backwards. She struggled before looking back to see two eyeless children, one on the right and the other the left, and they spoke in voices high enough to crack glass, "Our daddy did what your daddy did, but our daddy killed us, too. Wasn't he supposed to take you, too?" Then, suddenly their voices dropped to baritone. "You're next." They refused to let go of her wrists, holding on with the strength of body builders, so that no matter how hard Dina fought, she couldn't get away. She wrestled with all of her might until they finally disappeared. Her wrists were free.

Dina bolted back toward the bedroom door, but the children suddenly appeared again beside her on each side, banging on the door, mimicking her calls for her dead mother while laughing hysterically.

"Mommy! He's gonna kill us again!" they laughed as they slammed the door shut each time Dina opened it, explaining to her, "You can't get out. If Daddy doesn't want you out, you can't leave. See." The whole room turned into a sea of doors with identical peepholes.

Dina reverted to the center of the bedroom and placed her hands over her face, breaking down into a barrage of confusion before all the noise ceased.

"It's time to say good-bye, Dina," stated a woman's voice that was identical to her mother's, as lethally strong arms tightened their grip around her small frame.

"You're hurting me," she cried as the arms tightened around her like a python. As Dina's body became fatigued and weakened from being squeezed, the woman who was killed in the peephole stood beside her. She was inches from Dina's face ominously repeating, "It's gonna be okay. It's time to say good-bye."

"Wake me up!" she screamed, but the problem was that she wasn't dreaming. It was all real, and as she struggled to get away and the children danced around her, she finally collapsed into the man's arms out of breath, having become completely jaded and disoriented by intoxicating fear.

CHAPTER 9

The morning crept in with the birds unceremoniously quiet. Grace had almost overslept because her alarm failed to sound. She rushed around to prepare for work with an uneasy feeling lingering about in her spirit and believed that it had to do with the unresolved argument between her and Dina.

Dina was all she had, but she didn't know what to do when her daughter was showing all the signs of her father's mental illness. The only thing she could do was force her to go to therapy in hopes that before she left home for college, she would be okay.

Finally, showered and dressed, she stepped from the bathroom and approached Dina's bedroom door. She placed her hand on the knob but changed her mind about opening the door. Instead, she called her by name.

"Dina. Dina, baby, do you want to join me for breakfast before I leave for work?" If it was a mental illness, she didn't want to create even more confusion by forcing her will upon her when she could have been clearly distraught. "Dina," she called again before lightly knocking. She waited, walked away from the door to boil some water for her tea and oatmeal and took a deep breath of patience before returning to Dina's bedroom door, opening it and walking inside. Dina wasn't in the bed. She moved to the closet which was wide open, but Dina wasn't in there either.

"Oh my Lord," she whispered, throwing her hand against her chest as she gasped to catch her breath. "Dina? Dina!" Grace ran into the living room and out the front door barefoot shouting her daughter's name at the top of her lungs. As the door swung open behind her, it slammed against the wall only to bounce back off as the family of four cheerfully watched from inside the peephole, allowing Dina to watch, muffled, terrified and missing.

"I don't know where she is," she stated as she paced back and forth, having returned back inside. "I mean I woke up this morning, and she wasn't even in here. I checked the window, and it's locked, so she had to have left from the front door." She continued listening as patiently as she could while the police officer on the telephone asked her questions that she thought she'd already answered. "She didn't run away. She … she … she went to her room last night, and I went to bed. For all I know, she could have left right after I went to sleep. The point is that she isn't at home, and I can't go to work. I just got this job, and I need to find my daughter." There was another pause before Grace erupted. "You want me to go ahead and go to work and hope that she will be back home later?" Grace slammed the phone down and burst into tears, her mind racing. As she thought of every possible solution to the dilemma, she finally thought of Michael.

Grabbing her purse after searching high and low for a phone number to no avail, she drove through the entire community. She knew what Michael's car looked like, and that was going to be her target. She needed to determine where he lived so that she could question him about the possible whereabouts of her daughter. For all she knew, Dina could have gotten so angry at her that she fled to his home. Despite the fact that wouldn't be what she wanted, she hoped that was the case.

She circled all the blocks twice until she laid eyes on what she thought was Michael's car, but she wasn't certain which condo he lived in. Therefore, she pulled up behind the car, waited for a while, and finally exited her car, shouting his name so loudly that he was bound to hear her and come out.

It took no time for window blinds to start cracking and doors to start opening. Finally after about five minutes, the teenager walked outside with his mother trailing him, clearly provoked. Grace failed to consider how she may appear to his parents, and immediately addressed her, not him, with tears in her eyes and her arms open wide to ease the appearance of confrontation.

"My name is Grace, and my daughter is missing. We just moved here, and I just need to ask Michael if he'd seen her. I had no other way to get in contact with him…or you. I'm just desperate. Please forgive me, but I got no one else to ask."

She gave Grace a once over, but before she unleashed her fury, Michael spoke, "Ma, it's the mother of the girl I told you about."

Straight away, whatever the woman was about to say never escaped her mouth, but instead, she turned back, rushing back inside her home, shaking her head and waving her hands at her side like she wanted something to stop bothering her, but in an instant, she began storming back towards her. She grabbed Grace's arms, shaking them viciously while yelling, "Didn't my child tell you to get outta there already? Didn't he? Answer me!"

Grace broke away as Michael tried to calm his mother, but he couldn't. She jumped back into Grace's face before lowly uttering the words in a sick giggle, "Check the peephole. Michael told me what your daughter told you, and she was right." Then, she backed away, her grin transforming into a frown. "Let's go, Michael."

"But, Mom," he started, sympathetic to Grace who stood there without any answers.

"I said let's go now!"

He finally followed his mother into their home, leaving Grace in the middle of the street as everyone who'd peeped out to see the commotion, shut their blinds and curtains.

She got back in her car and raced home, rehearsing all of what Michael's mom said, and how her own daughter vaguely mentioned the people inside the peephole multiple times to her. Could that really have been the reason behind all of Dina's acting out? Was there really some truth to the superstition? All she wanted was Dina. She couldn't think about anything else except getting her back.

Dropping her keys at the front door, she rushed to gather them from the ground, but a large spider crawled atop her hand. She knocked it off and watched it run away. Shaken by it slightly, she inspected her hand, went to retrieve the keys once more and burst through the front door, out of breath. She called Dina's name, but got no answer before she turned to face the peephole. There it was staring back at her until there was a noise behind her.

"Dina?" she called, "Dina, is that you, sweetheart?"
She moved back into the hallway, first checking Dina's bedroom before fleeing to the bathroom and then her own room before coming back into the living room. It was then that she heard the odd noise again, as if someone was humming or trying to say something but hindered. She couldn't make out from what direction it came, so she stood very still until she realized it came from the front door.

Immediately, everything Dina, Michael and his mom told her rushed back into her memory, and as she took a deep breath, she approached the peephole. Her mind raced with thoughts that made no sense and a fear that had no real source. It was just there, creating a rush of adrenaline until...

"Mom?"

Grace spun around to see her daughter eerily standing behind her with an empty expression, like she'd seen a ghost. "Dina? Dina," she stated relieved, engaging her in a full embrace. "Where were you? What happened? I just looked in here for you. Where did you come from?" As she continued to ask a series of questions while checking her over, making certain that she wasn't scarred and hurt in any way, she noticed that Dina wasn't attempting to answer any of her questions. Then, she knew something was wrong. "Dina?"

She took a step back. Her daughter was staring back at the peephole again. Grace slowly turned around to do the same, wondering what her daughter was seeing that she simply couldn't. As she stared inside from a distance, all was blank. Therefore, she began to walk forward, deciding to engage with all the superstitious talk.

When her right eye met with the peephole, she waited, her breathing dwindling to light puffs as she moved to unconsciously hold her breath. It was then that a full newspaper clipping floated towards her eye, and she quickly backed away. She opened the door, but nothing was there. She turned back to Dina standing there as motionless as a pillar of salt. She shut the door once again, and peered back into the peephole. The newspaper was flattened against the hole this time, and she read it clearly.

It was the story of a murder-suicide that took place in condo address one hundred three, where the man took the life of himself and his entire family a long time ago. The font on the newspaper began to transform into a handwriting, and it scribbled the numerical address of the murder-suicide over and over again until the newspaper article flew away.

It was then that another article surfaced against the peephole with a clear picture of the entrance of the building when it was first built. According to the pictures on the paper, the address numbers used to be clearly visible on the outer brick as well as on the doors. The murder-suicide didn't take place in the condo across the hall. Grace became struck with fear.

She backed away from the door slowly pondering the address of her residence. It was one hundred one, but it wasn't originally. According to the paper, her address used to be one hundred three, the actually address of the murder-suicide. The addresses were switched.

"Dina...Dina...baby. This isn't one hundred one. This was the place. This was the place. I see what you saw," she continued, hyperventilating as she digested that the murder-suicide took place in her very home. "The addresses were switched. They were really switched. Why would they do that, Dina? When?"

Staring back in terror at the peephole, she yelled, "Dina, it's real. Get your things, and let's go. Dina..." she called, not taking her eyes off the peephole. "Dina!" she called again, reaching back with her hand attempting to grab her daughter. "We have to go." However, when she didn't feel Dina immediately behind her, she turned around.

There was Dina, but she wasn't alone. Standing six feet away from her were the two eyeless children at the beginning of the hallway. Their heads were tilted in order to peer around Dina's body to focus on Grace.

"We can still see you," the children giggled, pointing to their eye sockets. "It's our little trick." Grace stumbled backwards onto the front door at the sight of them, but as for Dina, Grace watched as she lifted her arms in a welcoming embrace of her mother like everything was normal. Meanwhile, the room full of others joined, standing there just as solemn as her daughter. The only two smiling were the eyeless children who greeted Grace with a warm welcome and incomplete explanation of everything going on with Dina.

"We told my daddy that we liked her, so he took her for us to play with, but she wanted you to come, too. She kept calling for you, so daddy said okay...because we aren't going anywhere. You aren't either."

It was then that Grace became overwrought with despair as she ran to snatch Dina from the bowels of the people who crowded around, but when she did, everyone in the room behind Dina lifted their fingers to their mouths, opened their eyes wide and said, "Shh." At that moment, a man and woman appeared behind her. The woman's arm was interlocked with the man's as they greeted Grace with tears flowing down their cheeks.

Dina calmly addressed her terrified mother. "Let go of me, mom. Stop screaming. Please let go of me."

Grace was ready to fight her way through any and everyone, however, when she saw the weeping couple, she became distraught as their tears began to somehow change. She moved closer to Dina as their tears formed a large concave lens that overtook the area between them and the couple. Grace touched clear formation and realized that it wasn't liquefied like tears are supposed to be, but solid. The tears were turning to glass.

"Dina, baby?" she asked confused.

"It's the peephole, mom. We're in it, and we're not getting out."

Once the truth registered, Grace began to beat the concave glass that shown through into her condo. The couple other the other side of it continued to weep, standing there watching her fight the glass that she would never exit until they vanished, leaving Grace to conclude her life in vivid memories of where she was to start fresh, where her daughter was supposed to celebrate her graduation from high school, the place that was supposed to be their new beginning, the place that was meant to be her home.

Finally, slumping to the floor like a ragdoll after minutes of brawling with the unbreakable bubble, she concluded her tantrum by taking the instruction of all the others that were still behind her with their mouths still covered with their index finger, who had instructed her to be quiet. Dina, who'd already screamed herself into a delirium all night, tiptoed over to her ailing mother who had seemed to have lost all sanity as she wobbled from side to side on the floor, knocking her head softly against the thick glass. She leaned over her mother before taking a seat beside her.

Dina grabbed her mother's hand which dangled onto the floor like it had no life left. She clasped her fingers inside her mother's, and she began to mimic her mom's actions, softly banging her head on the concave glass while caressing her thumb.

"Mom?"

Her mother stopped knocking her head at the sound of Dina's voice. A smile covered her face, but she continued staring ahead as Dina spoke. "This will still be our home ... just forever. Maybe Daddy wasn't crazy after all...just trapped."

Solemnly, Grace slightly dropped her head and faced her lovely daughter. A lone tear traced the sorrow of her high cheekbone and then escaped into the crevice of her lips before her mind chose hysteria over silence. Dina held her hand and watched along with all the others who were trapped with them inside the peephole.

CHAPTER 10

Ten Years Later

"Welcome, to our new home!" the proud father laughed as his wife and teenage twins, two boys, entered their brand new home. It was the first stop in a bumpy journey for them after having lost their previous place to live due to a fire.

He and his wife stood in the center of the living room ecstatic about their new lease on life while the children ran all around the place like it was a mansion. They kissed and embraced each other, but as his wife relaxed her head on his chest, she laid eyes on an old woman standing just within the doorway of the front door.

"Excuse me? Ma'am, may we help you?"

Her husband quickly looked toward the door and walked over to the old lady. "Yes ma'am, what can we do for you?"

"Do you live here now?"the old lady asked.

"Brand new in the neighborhood. Name's Wilcox, and this is my wife Brenda. It's nice to meet you, Miss…"

"Clance. I took my husband's last name like was normal back in my time. Now, you do what you want to, I suppose. My husband's dead now," she explained, peeping around them as she watched the children running and playing, "And so will you be if you stay."

Feeling threatened, the wife shouted, "What? Get away from here! How dare you threaten us!"

"It's not a threat, sweetheart. It's reality."

Instead of listening to anything else, the wife reached over and slammed the door in her face. "She has some nerve, Wilcox."

"Tell me about it."

There was another knock on the door, but before his wife opened it, he blocked her hand. "Let me handle this." He opened the door and started to speak but halted. There was no one there.

"Didn't you hear a knock?"

"I thought I did?"

"Guess we're hearing things already."

"I guess we are, huh? First a crazy old bat and now our hearing," she laughed.

As the door shut, the people inside the peephole watched the new family live their new wonderful lives until all good things come to an end when one looks through the peephole.

THE END

Thank you for your purchase. Feel free to leave a review and enjoy other Akirim Press (akirimpress.com) books which span a multitude of genres, or categories, both fiction and non-fiction. Below is a list to assist you in making your next entertaining selection.

Historical Fiction

CURSE THE COTTON
THE SECRET NOVEL COLLECTION
THE DAY I MET FREEDOM
DISGUISED BY A RAGING SMILE
GRANDMA'S GUN

Horror/Suspense
I THOUGHT I WAS ALONE TRILOGY
INSIDE THE GATES OF DOONS

THE TRUSTED
THE PEEPHOLE

Urban
I WILL DO ANYTHING FOR HER
MOST WANTED FELON
COLD BLOODED GOONS
THE GABRIEL'S TRAILS MURDERS SINS &
DECPETION BOX SET
HE BEATS ME
WHATEVER IT TAKES
LOVE, LIES & LIPSTICK
THE BEST KEPT SECRETS
WHEN IT COMES AROUND
UGLY

Dystopian
EXECUTION'S KARMA

Christian Thriller
AN EVIL WAS BORN

Poetry
GHETTO EYES
VERSE

Noir
FIRST DEGREE SINS
DEAD MAN'S MAYHEM

Romance
SINGLE AGAIN
AIN'T QUITE WHAT I THOUGHT!

AIN'T QUITE WHAT I THOUGHT 2!
DIGGIN' GOLD

Children's

WHEN I GROW UP, I WANT TO BE LIVING

PROOF!